I0579028

Thistle Bones

Tod Wiley Donaldson

KITSAP PUBLISHING

Thistle Bones
First edition, published 2020

By Tod Wiley Donaldson

Book Layout by Reprospace, LLC
Book Cover Images by Benjamin-Kaufmann, Obi-Onyeador from Unsplash
Author Photo Michael Lafferty

Copyright ©2020, Tod Wiley Donaldson

ISBN-13 Paperback: 978-1-952685-18-7

This is a work of fiction. Names, characters, businesses, places, events and incidents are either the products of the author's imagination or used in a fictitious manner. Any resemblance to actual persons, living or dead, or actual events is purely coincidental.

All rights reserved. No part of this book may be reproduced or transmitted in any form or by any means, electronic or mechanical, including photocopying, recording or by any information storage and retrieval system, without written permission from the author, except for the inclusion of brief quotations in a review.

Published by Kitsap Publishing
P.O. Box 572
Poulsbo, WA 98370
www.KitsapPublishing.com

Dedication

For Trish and Kevin Tierney,
Emily Nietupski, and the Laffertys.

Chapter 1

I remember it like yesterday, the first time I heard her sing. The room had been crowded, but most of them had gone – out to the deck that overlooked the water, to smoke and drink and hang out with the sweat-spangled t-shirts who had just rocked the place with their deeply laid hollow volume.

A weird and stale stillness hung over the restaurant and bar – but then a freshness, like an unshod horse, brought down from the hills, suddenly led into the barn, met our senses. The few of us who had stayed inside watched the untried filly climb up onto the stage, watched with cold eyes as she unslung her guitar, settled into the strap around her shoulders, and looked out over the microphone into the steely grey distance of the unknown – so close, breathing, farty, indifferent, arguing, grabbing their car keys, so close to leaving. So close, and yet so far away. Still tattooed by our dying echoes of the pounding drums and screaming guitars.

A few of us looked up. "Hi, I'm Nancy." She moved one foot to the left, nervously. "Not too many gals called Nancy anymore." She shuffled around again, then seemed suddenly to square her shoulders, and face the unquiet remnants of the crowd.

"My dad named me after his mom – my dad died in Vietnam – and that's what this song is about." A quick, sure-fire plunge of her right hand across the strings of her Martin D-8 guitar brought us all around to face her in stunned silence – the suspended F 9th chord hung in the air like a bell that had been waiting too long to be rung – and then she started to sing:

"Just when you least expect it, that's when the terrible twos come down.

And I forgot, and I neglected to mention that when you come around,

Just then you remembered to reject it, all of our twos were rolled up into one.

A fool who was running down the highway, looking for his Tuesday sun.

Tuesday sun, Wednesday run, never come back again, back again.

Then I remembered, oh, that's right, you reminded me

Nothing this good can last forever.

I looked back at you and something blinded me.

But I still can feel your leather in the Tuesday sun.

That reminded me, on Wednesday we'll run

Just behind us in the Tuesday sun,

We'll keep running, running, running

Until Wednesday's done.

We'll never come back again, at the Tuesday sun."

She stopped, her left hand on the fingerboard of her guitar, with one finger held depressed to chime the last single note ringing with her last sung syllable. And then she let it rest.

Well, let me tell you. The sweat boys had come in from the deck, and the girl's eyes were round. Nobody said a word. Then, suddenly, I shouted, "Shit! That's the stuff, if I've ever heard it." I started clapping so hard I thought my hands would fall off. I stood up, still clapping. And, of course – the whole place went into an uproar.

She shyly swiped at her hair, then spoke into the mic: "Thank you. You are so kind. Okay to play the rest of it?"

"YEP!" shouted big Deb, the barkeep and open-mic shepherd. "You go on ahead, girl."

"Ok, well, here."

"Like I said, the guy who inspired this with me is not here... Well, maybe he is. Let's see if we can call him up."

We all looked at each other and shrugged. Then the liquid chords chimed again, and the lovely waterfall of her voice drenched us –

"Every day is not wonderful,

And tomorrow's harder still.

But just because you're not pretty,

Doesn't mean you can't climb that hill.

I know there's a road that we walk together,

I know there's a road that we walk alone,
But if you ever want someone to walk with you,
I'm the one that you could walk home.
Every fool says the weather will change soon,
Just like a dollar bill.
And the faster they deny it,
They make more sense (just) standing still.
I know there's a song that you're born singing,
I know that you sing that song alone.
But if you ever want someone to sing with,
You know that I'm the girl who'll sing along.
I'm the girl to sign your songs."

The drunken, raucous applause was almost deafening, and I was a veteran of back-stage large venues. I got up and walked over to Big Deb.

"Who is she, Deb? What the hell is her name – Nancy? Christ, who the hell is named Nancy anymore? Think that's her real name?"

"I dunno, big Tom, but I'm gonna tell ya – you better snag this one quick, before she gets away. We don't see raw talent like that in this dump often, as if you didn't know."

"Right."

I rocked back on my heels and watched Nancy waving at the crow, mouthing "thanks" into the air, as she moved offstage. I slid over, of course, and intercepted her as she shakily came down the stairs.

"Hey! That was great! Really something – uh, could I ask you a few questions?"

"Well, sure, but you probably want to talk to my manager, Charlie, over there."

I looked over and saw the classic three-toned hustler, the bastard who was the bane of my existence, the guy who gave every music agent a bad name – a pimp in wolves' clothing, not even trying to hide his carnivorous and carnal intent. I looked back at Nancy, who by now was standing just a few paces behind me, backstage, as the next heavy-metal cover sweat group started to troop up the stairs that she had just walked down.

"Why, little lady! That sounded good! Did you really write them songs, all by yourself? Shit, I'll cover these with my partner Enrico here."

"Yeah," answered Nancy, auburn hair in a swirl around her face, eyes dancing with a mixture of joy and fear in the palpable lust of the situation. "I wrote 'em. But you guys couldn't cover them, not in a million years."

A dumb, stark, perturbed, and slightly angry look dropped over the faces of the metal dudes. "Why not, babe? Shit, we're about to be stars! We're heading to the Tacoma Dome, in case you don't know, you little bitch!"

"Yeah!" echoed the rest of the three choured dumbbells.

"You'd best know, when you're talkin' to your betters! YEAH, YEAH, YEAH! And don't be saying no shit about leathers, bitch, or we'll..."

"You'll what, you little chimp?" Suddenly, righteously, Nancy's manager, Charlie, was in the dude's face. Charlie had a grin like a church without a bell; he had a sinewy, fabricated grace like an empty highway. There was something scary about Charlie – even I could feel it. The dude couldn't have been more than 5'7", weight maybe 140 lbs – but the abrupt evilness was there, oh yeah – he brought it on. There was an implicit reality – if you wanted to fuck with it – you'd have to take it all the way. A Priori, baby, let's battle to the death. I love stupid little losers like you. I'm on you like a can on peas, like flies on shit, like too much mustard on an old Coney Island dog smothered in the sand. Gold glinted in his teeth, and some were missing as well – almost as if he had purposely left those gaps, to show that he was no stage pirate – he was the real deal.

He also reeked – I don't think that he'd bathed or washed the clothes he's been wearing in weeks, or even months. Or – even years.

He slid his leering grin over to me. "You like our girl, don't ya, big Tom?"

"You know who I am?"

"Oh yeah. Everybody in Icabod City knows you, as far as music goes. You got a pretty good rep. We know you're fair."

Charlie iced his eyes back to the dudes still hanging on the riser. "Hey, fuckheads. You wanna fuck with me and Little Rick?"

From the background of the back stage ether there suddenly appeared an apparition – Little Rick, the legendary stagehand roadie. As he loomed closer, his size became apparent, and also the cynical satire of his nickname – Little Rick stood 6'8" and weighed about 380 lbs. He was like a human elephant dressed in jeans and a tank top. His eyes gleamed hatefully out of a skull the size of a bowling ball.

"Throw down, little dudes," rumbled the Rickster.

The skilly skulls shook their heads and quickly ran up the steps to the stage.

Charlie gave me a slow, calculating look. Nancy stood behind him, quietly, packing up her gear and putting away her guitar. Before he could speak, I headed him off.

"Look, Charlie, I've never heard your girl, Nancy, play before. Shit, man, no one has – you can't expect us not to react if you just pull her out of the can and pop her on the stage out of nowhere."

"Hey, asshole!" Nancy was all up in my face, like a buzz saw. Her eyes were Indian, but her face was pale. She's part Indian, I thought. But, mostly white – and a strong white, at that. Maybe Irish, or Italian.

"I play where I want to play! I call the shots, not Charlie. He's only along for the ride. But you're right – I did just pop up here. It wasn't even scheduled, we're on our way to Cleveland, to open for the Bullhead Roosters – and then on to a gig in Wyoming, at a ski place, or something."

"There ain't no ski places in Wyoming featuring music in the summer," I said, eyeballing Charlie, watching to see if pulled a gun or a knife. He didn't.

"However, there is a blues-rock festival happening in Seattle that I could get you into—"

Charlie was in my face again. "Listen, Tom, I know damn well what you're trying to do. She's already got a manager, OK?" He looked around me at Nancy. "I'll be out in the van, sweetheart. Little Rick will stay here in case you need him."

Nancy hooked her arm in mine and led me out onto the deck. She lit a cigarette, and took an air-filled, long tug at it, holding in the smoke. Offering it to me, I realized it was a joint. What the hell, I rarely smoked the stuff anymore, but I took a hit anyway. The midnight clouds over the water deepened their colors; the reflections of the deck lanterns became more dazzling.

"Charlie used to be Charlene," she looked at me sideways, gauging my reaction. "She was my best friend in high school. The she got raped one night in the alley behind the local watering hole." She took another toke. "That when she started to turn, and she's been Charlie ever since. Couldn't tell, could you?"

I shook my head. "Hell, no. If somebody messed with her now…"

"Yeah, she'd cut their balls off. Listen, I appreciate your enthusiasm for my music, and I know the kind of connections you've got. There is no gig in Cleveland, and we're not even sure about this thing in Wyoming. I just said that stuff to cool you out, make you lay down your push, and back you off. I'm interested in the blues-rock festival – but you've got to go through her – I mean him – OK?"

"Sure. You guys aren't, you know, together, are you?"

"Nah. I'm just a regular, straight chick trying to make it, keep from working at McDonald's or the ski factory." She looked at me with appraising eyes, slightly slanted above her high cheekbones. "But in case you've got any ideas, you better check them at the door. I only go with other musicians, and very rarely, at that. I haven't had a steady dude since Robby moved up north and disappeared fishing in the Bering Sea – that's who that second song was for. Besides, aren't you a little old for me?" Her eyes twinkled above her smile.

"Well, I've got some news for you, Nancy. I play drums, bass, can sing a hearty tone, and blow blues harp with the best of them. Whatcha thinka that?"

"Hmmmmm," she murmured. "Is that right? Well, have another toke, fatso. As a matter of fact, keep it. I think Little Rick is getting concerned. We've been leaning on this railing for too long. I'm not the only act that he roadies for – but I am his favorite."

"Are you two, you know –"

"Hey, Tommy – don't push it – check into booking me into a four-song spread at that Seattle festival - call me. Big Deb has Charlie's numbers. Get hold of me through that, and we'll see if we can throw down together." A mischievous look crossed her countenance. "I'd like to hear you play – maybe we'll tour together. Call us, OK?"

She pushed away from the railing, spun around, and was gone in a swirl of talent and intelligence that I hadn't quite expected. This was no untried filly after all. No. This was a thoroughbred racehorse, standing tough in the stalls, waiting to spring out onto the full-length six furlong race – with all bets riding on a long shot.

And I planned to be one of the first ones up at the betting window. I was, after all, one of the best talent spotter on the west coast – hadn't I discovered and sold the prospecting careers of the Evil 88's, Sarah Pullinsky, Scott McBraid, Jimmy-Jam and the Blue Forks, Large River, the Toothpick Fairies, and Evil Mike and the Strange Backpackers? And what about Coalmine Jim? Hell, I was the best-known and most heavily regarded music agent in the Northwest. I was Big Tom Mooney, ex-cop (14 years as a rural, backwoods deputy with the county sheriffs), musical library collector (3,617 original LPs, 1,800 cassette tapes, 214 glass '78 albums, 218 items of autographs, photos, and backstage ephemera), and resident spy for emerging artists in small towns in the Northwest, including Washington, Oregon, Idaho, and Montana. However, since the garage band-grunge-flannel-Kurt Cobain wars – I hadn't been farther east than Spokane. There was plenty of talent coming out of the woods right here in Podunk, a small shipyard town next to Icabod City, which was just 16 miles away from Bremelo, where the shipyard laid its ships. Navy ships. Aircraft carriers. Nuclear. Nuclear fission, which fueled their ships in the 7th fleet, Pacific, unlike the ones I'd served on, which had been converted and then de-commissioned – the old diesels.

I wondered if Nancy had relatives serving in the Navy. And then, just as I heaved my bulk off the rail to turn around and go back inside, I had to wonder no more.

Chapter 2

The guy coming through the door out onto the deck was thirty-ish, dressed in an old blue pea coat, and hadn't shaved in at least three days. Either that, or just had a natural heavy 5 o'clock beard shadow. His intense eyes pierced into mine, and I immediately remarked the resemblance to his sister in his facial structure – high cheekbones, slightly slanted brown eyes, pale skin. He looked tired.

"Big Tom Mooney?" he asked.

"Yeah, who are you?"

"Franklin Opano. I'm Nancy's brother." He stuck out a wiry paw from the sleeve of his coat, and I clasped it in mine. There was an amazing strength there – and we held the grasp a little longer than was customary. His eyelids folded in an approving, pleasurable way as he let go of my hand.

"You mind if we stay out here and talk awhile? I've ordered us a couple of drinks."

Big Deb came bursting through the doors as he said this, bearing two fat bucket glasses, ice rattling in them. "OK – Big Tom's regular, Lemon Hart rum and Coke, and for you, stranger, Absolut straight up with a twist. That about right, fellas? OK then." She backed out with a wary look in her eyes directed at me. What's that about, I thought. Big Deb knows me better than anybody in five counties – she knows I can take care of myself.

Sole owners of the Tides Out Inn Bar and Grill, Big Deb and Big Tom – the two most solid names in the talent-spotting business. And yet – there was a warning in her eyes. I wondered how the cash intake at the bar was going. After all – I still owned 1/3 of it. The Low Tides Inn would never make us rich – but it just might sustain us.

I straightened up. "OK, Mr. Opano. You've got my undivided attention." I took a sip of the Lemon Hart. My God, I thought. That's good stuff.

My conversational participant/adversary did the same, smacked his lips, and sighed. "My God, that's good stuff," he said. "And you know what – it dies painless with me."

"Wait a minute. That's a line from… hang on, I'll get it in a second… that's a line from…"

"A movie, made from a book, written by Chandler – Raymond. 'Farewell, My Lovely.' The line was spoken by Jesse Florian, one of Robert Mitchum's informers, after he brought her a pint of gin to get her to talk. Ah, L.A. Don't you miss all that 1930s detective business, the beautiful sinful broads, the sleek automobiles, the gun molls? Don't you miss the Maltese Falcon?"

Big Tom took another slug off his drink and answered, "Now, that was Dashiell Hammet, and the characters were played by Bogie, Brigit O'Shaugnessy, Peter Lorrie, Caspar Goltman, and the young gunsell was played by – wait a minute, I'll get it – shit. What was his name?"

"Nope, big boy. Other than Bogie and Peter Lorrie, you've done nothing more than name the characters in the film by their character names. Bogart was Sam Spade, Sidney Greenstreths as Caspar Goltman, Peter Lorrie was Joe Cairo, ______ was Bridgit O'Shaughnessy, and Elisha Cook was the gunsell. But – come now, Mr. Tom. That is neither here nor there." Opano shifted his legs, crossing his right over his left.

"I have a proposition to make to you. Obviously, my sister is extremely talented. It is also obvious that this fact has, this evening, come to your notice. This 'Charlie', who purports to be her manager – well this little transsexual obviously has to go."

Opano tossed a hand over his shoulder. "And you must take the place of this, this, what shall we say, 'pretender'. Because that's all that this 'Charlie' character is, Mr. Tom. A pretender."

The dude leaned back in his deck chair and sipped his drink. He set it down. He folded his hands in a steeple, and looked at me over the steeple. I was prepared to be fucked with. I'd sent that look many times before. As he started to speak, over his carefully steepled hands, I cut the bastard off. I'd had enough of his posturing bullshit.

"So, what – you're Nancy's brother? Full blood brother?"

"Well, half-brother, actually. We…"

"OK, Jack. I know your name ain't Jack, but that's the name I use for fuckers who come to me with one kind of deal working. Listen – I just heard Nancy sing and play her tunes tonight for the first time, OK? OK. I was impressed. Everybody in Icabod City, for that matter, everybody in the surrounding five counties knows that I'm a musical talent scout – so whatever you're about to say, don't. No bribes, no bullshit, no talk about where you think her career should go, OK? And don't worry, I ain't got no hard-on for your sister. I just recognize talent when I see it on stage, and then I try to move it on down the line so that said talent gets a crack at making it big and I get my cut. OK? And I definitely saw that tonight. Now, I know that Charlie, or Charlene , or what-the-fuck-ever, is her so-called manager. And I know that Little Rick is guarding her, out of love, it would seem. But listen, Opano, I don't want to get up in your face with this, but I'll tell you – she is probably the most naturally talented singer/songwriter I've encountered in the last five years – and I would love to represent her, and live up gigs for her, venues in the area and beyond, and maybe get her signed to a major label – but not, I repeat, not if guys like you – her half-brother, which I can see is true – and guys like Charlie/Charlene are gonna fuck with me. You're Navy Intelligence, am I right?"

Big Tom leaned back, took a slug of his drink, and eyeballed Franklin Opano.

Opano took a sip off his own drink and eyeballed me back. "No, man. I've been out of the Navy for five years. Ranked out as a senior grade lieutenant, just short of a light commander. But you've got a pretty sharp eye, don't you? Look, Tom. Call me Franklin. Stop with the Opano shit. And, let me explain something. On my mother's side,

Nancy and I have quite a lot of American Indian blood – Suquamish, Skokomish, Nisqually. On my father's side, it's mostly Irish with a little Italian – out of New York."

Franklin leaned in towards me, accentuating the intensity of what he was about to say. "The New York connection is what I wanted to talk to you about, Mr. Mooney."

Mr. Mooney? Oh shit, here we go, I thought. Or rather, though Big Tom. Because I am out of the picture, for now, and Big Tom, Franklin, Jocelyn, Spreckles, Reginald, Oswald, and Nancy are in – for now.

"There is a little bit of a problem," Franklin said, leaning forward. "Apparently, after Nancy's aunt died last year – our parents died many years ago – Aunt Prudencia (Patty, Mattie's younger sister, the last of the elders in the Franklin clan) was Nancy's guardian – a will and trust was discovered. As the estate moved into probate court, the call went out to possible like-named relatives who might file a claim against the estate – it became clear that Nancy stood to inherit quite a lot of money in liquid and non-liquid assets bearing a value of two to three million dollars."

Franklin leaned back and took a drink. Big Tom pondered.

"Why the fuck are you telling me this? Opano? Franklin? What-the-fuck-ever your name is? What the fuck has this got to do with me?"

"Because I am convinced that other, more distant relatives of Nancy's and mine have surfaced, and are stalking her, even as we speak. I think that these relatives of the Opano clan, namely, my side of the family, seek to kill Nancy in a way that looks accidental, kill me outright as a member of law enforcement, and rush in to claim the estate."

"Yeah, a member of law enforcement. I knew I'd made you for a fed. I've got major connections in the Suquamish tribe, and I've never heard the name Opano – Franklin, however, I have. How about we switch – and I call you by your real name, Opano Franklin?"

He shrugged. "OK, like I said, I knew you for a good eye. It is Opano Franklin – yeah. We are a family from that clan – what's left of it."

"Doesn't Opano mean 'lamb chop' or something?"

Opano laughed. "It used to mean 'pork chop' in an old slang idiom that no one uses anymore. It's a nickname. We all had nicknames. Nancy's was 'Thistlebone'."

"Thistlebone?"

"Yep. She liked to run around in the woods. One day she got into a big thistle patch, down by a creek, and came home covered with the things. Our mom undressed her, and while she was pulling them out of her hair, Nancy asked her, 'What you call these things, Mama?' Mom told her, 'Thistles. You're all covered with thistles, right down to your bones, you little Thistlebones.' So we all started calling her that. That's how I got my name. I loved pork chops – couldn't get enough of 'em," he chuckled. "Luckily, my Uncle Pete was a hog farmer – we always had plenty of 'em around. And by the way, call me Opo, Big Tom. That's a nickname for my nickname."

"OK, Opo. And just call me Tom, OK? I know that Deb and me are both large humans, but the 'big' stuff gets old. Especially when somebody like 'Little' Rick crosses your path. You know?"

They both laughed and Big Deb stuck her head out the side door.

"Another round, fellas?" Her eyes glinted when they fell on Tom's who was facing her, his back to the bay.

"Yeah, darlin'. Make 'em doubles. We're gonna be here awhile. I got a lot of fat to chew with old Porkchop here."

Deb shook her head and went back inside. Opo's back was to her and didn't see the gesture, but I could tell – he knew. His eyes held the same hard, remorseless glitter.

"Alright, Opo. What the hell is with this estate stuff, and you and Nancy? What's the element of danger I'm sensing here? And what the fuck does it have to do with an old, fat talent scout?"

Opo leaned forward. "You ever heard of a dude named Spreckles?"

Chapter 3

Oh yeah, I'd heard of Spreckles. Hell, I'd arrested him three times in the last two decades. He was a low-life legend around Icabod City. He'd come out of the swamps, literally, and begun to wreak havoc in Nipsac County. By the time he was 12 years old, he'd been in juvenile holding pens about ten times, in custody for any number of stupid, animalistic activities – throwing shit, I mean actual human feces, at the rural route mailman; leaving evil, handwritten words of a threatening nature on sidewalks and school walls (this was way back – before graffiti); screaming obscenities at families picnicking by the waterside. He'd been looked at by all the mental health experts, been interviewed. He had a clean bill of health. His dad was a fireman, his mother worked as a checker at the local market, his one brother (Oswald) and one sister (Jocelyn) were nice regular kids. Since his mother was half Suquamish Indian, making him a ¼ tribal member, and he had been born and raised on the Port Madison reservation, the tribe finally said that if released into their custody, they'd try to straighten him out. They gave him a job – counting fish in creeks and rivers during the salmon runs. He liked it, and settled down. After a while, he even wore a uniform – blue cap, with the tribal insignia patch, brown shirt, and blue trousers. He lived in a shack up in the Poolsak Hills, on a two-acre spread deeded by the tribe to their family as a 99-year lease. All was well. It seemed that Spreckles (so nicknamed because he was often found as an infant snout-deep into the family bag of sugar) had finally found his niche.

Just before I quit law enforcement, I was patrolling around the edges of the Suquamish reservation boundaries, when a call came over the radio.

Chapter 4

"Car 119, Suquamish Tribal Police report possible felony disturbance action, request backup – proceed to Poolsak Hills, residence – contact neighbors standing in road, be advised subject reported armed with shotgun, shots fired. Switch to Tribe frequency and coordinate response."

I went roaring down Nooksack Road, lights and siren. I thumbed the sender on my mic.

"Nipsac County Car 119, Mooney responding. Calling nearest tribal unit, over."

"Yeah, Tom, this is Tribal Unit 7, Paul Louie. I'm two minutes out from contact. We've got reported shotgun blasts, maybe even a hostage."

"Paul, let's meet at the bottom of the hill. Where's backup?"

"Units 9 and 11 four minutes out. We woke up the chief."

It was about 4 a.m. I knew Chief Bigelow – on a situation like this, he'd be moving quick. I called in to my dispatcher.

"Dispatch, Car 119. Coordinating with Tribal Units 7, 9, and 11 regarding Poolsack Hill incident. Tribal chief advised and involved. Two minutes to hook-up."

I careened around the long curve to the junction with the Poolsak road, and saw Paul Louie's unit, blue and red lights flashing, just pulling in. We jumped out and put our heads together.

"Whatcha got?"

My whole body was flooded with adrenaline. The huge, forested hills above us were as dark and cold as a witch's tit.

"I don't know for sure, Big Tom, but I think it's Spreckles. His neighbors down the road called first – you know – the ones leasing the Sigally spread?"

"Yeah, I know 'em. The Robinsons. Old time tribal, never bother nobody."

"Right, but they're scared shitless now, man. Bill Robinson's called his two sons, and they're on their way here from Kingston. Plus, old lady Mathilda's up there. And she's armed to the teeth."

"Shit, that old gal's crazy. If we're not careful, she could take us all out. Where the hell is…"

Just then, Tribal Units 9 and 11 came screaming around the bend, lights blazing. They bucketed in and came to a stop next to us, jumping out and forming up. Now we had a command post. Legally, since it was on a tribal reservation, Paul Louie was in command – senior officer on the scene. 9 and 11 were Borkam Jones and Chip Two-Horse. They all looked at me.

"Look, Officer Louie – it's your call. Do we wait for command to arrive, or go up there now? Any more calls from 911?"

My radio crackled. It was the chief of the Suquamish police, Billy Worthman. "Big Tom, you there? Over."

"Yeah, Billy, I'm here at the Poolsack Road upgrade, with Tribal Units 7, 9, and 11. We await command structure, over."

"Nature of incident indicated full interdiction. Possible hostage, I've heard. We've got to make contact with the neighbors who originally called in the complaint before we move in. Have you requested outside backup? Over."

"Negative, Chief. I let county know the sit-rep. Awaiting your advice as to a roll-out call. Over."

"Call 'em out, Big Tom. At least two units, and possibly a SWAT team. You know Mathilda's up there."

'Batty' Matty, as we all knew her, was the chief's sister. It made for a touchy situation. She was a tribal activist, often in the news, and was said to be armed to the teeth. She'd buried her husband behind her cabin four years ago, against tribal law. But nobody fucked with Mattie.

"Ah, OK, Chief. What's your 20?"

"I'm ten minutes out. You know where I live, who's in 9 and 11? I know 7."

"9 is Borkam Jones, 11 is Two-Horse. Over."

"OK, let's put you and Two-Horse in charge of the command post you've established. Put 7 out on the curve ¼ mile back to set up a preliminary roadblock. Anybody driving this time of night is either drunk, running drugs, or crazy. Shit – now it's starting to rain like hell."

Sure enough, a giant black dog of a cloud camped out in the sky 200 feet above our position, and let loose. An evil wind blew the rain sideways into our faces.

"OK, Chief. 7 is on the way to roadblock, and 9 and 11 are gearing up with vests and shotguns. We're getting the rain, too. What's your ETA?"

"Four minutes now, Big Tom. I'm trying to get Mathilda on the horn."

"Uh, Chief – I thought she didn't have a telephone."

"That's a rog. I gave her a cell phone last year. Only I know the number."

A dull, cracking boom went off 1000 feet above us. It was followed quickly by two lesser, sharper cracking sounds.

"Gunfire on the Ridge! Gunfire on the Ridge!" Borkam Jones was signing his mic so quickly, nothing was getting through.

"Cool it, Jones, I've got it." I keyed my mic.

"Chief – we've got gunfire on the ridge – sounded like one shotgun, followed by two pistol shots. Please advise."

"Call in your horses, Tom. I'll be there in two minutes."

"Dispatch, this is Nipsac County Deputy Car 119, Patrol Sergeant Mooney, on tribal assistance call, Suquamish Reservation, incident location Poolsak Hills Road Junction. Have established official contact with tribal police, am authorized to request under full county command two additional patrol units and a SWAT team backup. Weapons fired, repeat, weapons fired. No engagement by officers at present. We are in a holding pattern. T.P.C. is two minutes out. Awaiting contact with origin of complaint. Hostage situation possible. Tribal elders and the blood sister of T.P.C. are involved. Request advice from watch commander and legal regarding reservation tactics and interaction. I am in a holding pattern, until advice and backup arrive. Over."

"Car 119, message received. Am seeking advice and command. Wait one."

Mooney waited. Two-Horse and Jones looked at him, blinked, and looked up at the huge hog-back ridge that loomed above them, pitch black in the ageless dark.

"Tribal 7, this is Big Tom. How's your sitch? Over."

"Big Tom, this is 7. I am 5 by 5 and squared away. Unit is blocking both lanes and I am situated 40 feet from collision danger. Over."

"Tribal 7, outstanding. Hold current position and stay alert. Command decision imminent. Be advised that county backup with full attack and defend squad will be coming down that road in one-half hour – and also be advised that armed perps could at any time nail your position. Light up your unit – all spotlights and flashers. Copy? Over."

"Tribal 7, copy, Tom. Unit lit – I'm safe and have a direct line of fire. My sidearm is cleared, charged, and ready for take-off. Hey – didn't I just hear more shots up on the ridge?"

As he spoke, we heard the gunfire. As before, yet in reverse – two small pistol reports, then one boom of a shotgun.

"Affirmative, 7. I'm going to reinforce your position ASAP. Meanwhile, stay concealed. Will advise. Out."

Two-Horse was standing next to me, weapon cleared of his holster and double fisted, staring up into the gloom. Jones was in a similar position, all of us ducked down behind our vehicles. I looked down and was surprised to see my own service pistol out of my holster. I quickly stuck it back in.

"Listen, you guys, don't get too jumpy. It's probably just Spreckles going nuts in the moonlight, had too much to drink, firing at the deers and bears walking around his cabin..."

"Ain't no moonlight. Clouds and rain," said Jones, nervously fingering his handgun.

"Spreckles don't drink no more, neither," chimed in Two-Horse. "And, he's got a shotgun. Who the hell is firing off that pistol?"

"Well, it's probably Mathilda... Chief Bigelow will know what to do."

Just then, the chief's cruiser came rocketing around the bend, lights flashing off the trees. He got his 230 lb frame out of the vehicle, his trusted sidekick Officer Ben "No Gloves" Glover coming out the other side. Ben adjusted his tight, black gloves. His nickname, "No Gloves", was reverse psychology by the locals.

"OK, Tom. Give me a situation report and a plan of action. You know that my sister's up there. Is it Spreckles or did Mattie do this shit just to get in the news?"

"Unknown, Chief. I've called in major county backup. We've got 7 on a vehicle roadblock lit up ¼ mile up the roadway. Suggest he be reinforced immediately by Unit 11. I mean, right now, Chief."

Bigelow nodded. "Reinforce Unit 7, Jones. Double up the roadblock and be prepared to lay down spike strips. You got 'em?"

Jones nodded affirmative. "Shotguns out?" he asked.

"Yep. We don't know what the fuck this is about, but let's be ready for anything. Shotguns out, full ready kill rounds. Await command advisement. Stay off the road and concealed. Make sure your vehicles are doubled up to create a no-fly zone. Above all – stay on the air."

"Right, Chief." Joes dug rubber and went off to join 7.

"Tom, I can't get ahold of my sister." Chief Bigelow's eyes were enormous, dark brown and reflective of the forests of the Indian night. "What the fuck do you think we should do?"

"Well, Chief – let's send your next tribal unit down the other way, and affect a vehicle roadblock there. Then we'll have it penned, until the county gets here. Meantime – me and Two-Horse could do a little scouting expedition."

I looked over at Two-Horse, who grinned and nodded vigorously.

"After all – I trained him. He's like a son to me – except, he farts a lot."

Two-Horse gave a low, chortly laugh, switched his service weapon from his right hand to his left and back again, and farted loudly.

"Especially when he's about to come under fire from hostile elements. Chief – here's the way I see it. Me and Two-Horse go up there, vests and shotguns and extra clips for our nines. You guys mill around down here, make noise, get on the bullhorn, tell whoever the fuck it is firing weapons up there to surrender. Major county firearms teams should

18

be here in twenty minutes. Meantime, me and Two-Mules can flank this fuck-whoever-it-is and at best be in a position to take him out if he decides to get in our gunsights. Whaddya think?"

Bigelow's forehead cascaded into a furrowed tumble, as he mulled it over.

"OK, Tom. You and Two-Horse. Put your radios on touch contact only – key once for in position – key twice for in danger – key three times for hold fire. That way you can approach and conceal with no voicemail. If you take hostile fire, return fire and take the suspect out – you have my authority. But watch for hostages. If he's in a house, try to get him out. What about tear-gas flangers?"

"Yeah, Chief. Give us each four of those."

Chief Bigelow motioned to No Gloves, who quickly popped the trunk of the command cruiser and began handing Two-Horse tear-gas canisters. I walked over and took the firing unit and slung it over my shoulder. It was surprisingly light – I hadn't had one of these slung in years. The gas canisters, the mechanism to fire them – they were all made of a lightweight plastic. Kind of like a lot of people I knew.

But – not the ones on this reservation. It wasn't just the fact that my mother had been born there – I had a connection to these people that was deeper than that. And they knew it – knew what it was – all the way from Bartram Jones up at the roadblock, to my old friend Two-Horse, standing next to me, geared up for combat and farting like a bandit in a cheese parade, to Myron George "Big-Horn" Bigelow, Chief of the Suquamish Tribal Police, whom I'd known all my life. When we were kids, we used to wrestle down on the sandy beach. And now we were in combat preparation mode again. Just like in 'Nam.

Another story.

"Sergeant Mooney, are you ready to proceed? I am officially taking command of this operation at this time, 0500 hours. Do you concur?"

"I concur and agree, Tribal Chief Bigelow. I stand relieved of incident command post. I will proceed forthwith under your orders."

"Very well, Sergeant Mooney. Nipsack County has been advised, as per tribal law, you are under my command at this moment and forthwith. Proceed as planned under my orders. Advance under fire to attempt to subdue civilian hostile and relieve any hostages under his or her control forthwith – full rules of engagement are authorized – approach, extend, conceal, and fire as needed. I now release you and Two-Horse to operate in a full combat trail mission under Suquamish Tribal Law. Are you now, have you ever been, a member of the Suquamish Tribe?"

"Yes I am, yes I have, yes, I always will be until I die."

"Two-Horse Car-Wrecker, are you now, have you ever been a member of the Suquamish Tribe?"

"Yes I am, yes I have, and always I will be until I die."

"Then, as a duly and righteously appointed and descended chief of the Sealth, Suquamish Nation, I now acknowledge you both as full-blooded warriors, to go forth and defend this tribe against your enemies. Now, move out."

Me and Two-Horse immediately split up – he went right, I went left. There was a windy dirt road leading up to the Poolsak Ridge – after the first curve, the tree line dropped into a 160-foot deep gully. That was on Two-Horse's side. On my side, I had gravel-edged hillsides going up about 80 feet, and then suddenly dropping back to level out with the road. The rain was slacking off, but the wind was picking up, and getting colder. I said, "Fuck it," and dropped out of concealment after the second curve brought us farther up into darkness.

Two-Horse emerged from the trees, dragging himself over the edge of the road. I motioned him over to me.

"Fuck it, man. Let's just walk up the road – you tight behind me, both on the left. Watch for sudden vehicles, coming down without headlights, and for godssakes, watch above us on the hog back for defilade fire. I'll cover level, you cover overhead ambush – got it, Horse?"

He nodded. He farted, softly.

"Goddammit, Horse – nix on the farts. I love you, Two-Mule, but it could get us killed. Watch up and watch six – got it?"

He nodded and we walked up the road, trying not to scrunch the gravel beneath our combat boots too loudly. I had a Lifesaver in my mouth, a butterscotch one. I was hoping that it would work. It was like hoping that I'd win the lottery. In other words, as me and Two-Horse walked up the next curve in that road, toward the lights of a house and outbuildings, I expected to die at any minute.

And I knew, so did he.

We rounded the curve, walking out of the dark in to the floodlights of a hillside pig-farm operation. The command post was one and a half miles below. We'd been walking for 45 minutes.

"Shit, Two-Horse."

We'd halted just before the floodlights of the house and barn could illuminate us.

"We'll have to go back into the trees and flank the structures. Remember the key codes the chief told us to use on the radio. No talking, and no squawking. Weapons ready."

"Big Tom, what the fuck?" whispered Two-Horse. "Why don't we just wait for a helicopter, withdraw to a firing sight? Why we got to go in? Shit – we don't even know who's who, here."

I thought. "You're right, Two-Horse." I thought some more, then softly patted his shoulder. It was like patting a granite rock. "You're right, for now, my old farting mule friend. I'll key the chief."

I keyed once for: in position. Then I waited five seconds, and keyed three times for: hold fire. And just as Two-Horse and I were about to disengage, all hell broke loose.

Chapter 5

Out of one of the larger barn-type buildings came Spreckles, stumbling out as if pushed, and coming to a standing rest with his hands up. He was obviously terrified. He was dressed in blue jeans, sneakers, and a t-shirt with a tribal patched fish-watcher windbreaker. He stood in the floodlights shining from the large barn to his right, and blinked.

"Hey, you crazy bitch!" he shouted. "I didn't do nothin' – nothing!"

He saw the black snout of a double-barreled shotgun sticking out from the door he'd been pushed from. Nothing more. Then a cold, deadly voice spoke.

"Listen, Circhuteni, Chiquitite. I can't believe we took you in, into this sacred tribe, into my place. You should die, now."

"No!" screamed Spreckles. Suddenly he took off running, right towards our position. The shotgun boomed, and Spreckles went down.

Shit, I thought. Mattie just killed Spreckles. Now there'll be hell to pay. I yelled out "Spreckles! Run this way! We've got you covered!"

Mattie had let off the right barrel into Spreckles upper shoulder area; he was still alive, but staggering. He fell 40 feet in front of me just as Mattie swung the remaining barrel around to face me and Two-Horse.

"What the fuck are you two half-breeds doing up here?" she yelled. "This is a tribal matter, and I'm a tribal elder! And let me kill this worthless pea-hen!"

Spreckles was down, bleeding. I watched him crawling, feeling his way towards a small ditch that might give him cover.

I swung my gun sight on Mattie as she walked out of the barn, crazy as a loon, mad as a hatter, and righteous as only an aging tribal elder can be.

Suddenly a large voice boomed out behind me, "STOP! Stop, I say! You STOP in the name of the Suquamish Nation!"

It was Chief Bigelow, Mattie's brother. After giving us our order to re-con the hill, he'd handed off command and been right behind us the whole time.

Only an Indian could do that.

"Mattie! Drop the gun! Your hunted is down, repeat, my girl – you have dropped your prey! Don't be crazy! Here I come – are you gonna shoot me, Chit-a-Meienteichi? Your own brother?"

Mattie stopped, lowered her shotgun, and looked at Bigelow.

Me and Two-Horse stood in the darkness beyond the lights, like we were watching a stage play. I kept my nine-millimeter trained on Mattie, however. I wasn't gonna let my old friend get gunned down by a crazy old woman.

Two-Horse farted, quietly.

Suddenly Bigelow went rigid, staring at the figure back-lighted in the barn door.

"That is not my sister." He stared another five seconds, then turned to look at me. "Did you hear me, Tom? That, is not, my, sister."

The woman standing in the door let off her left barrel, and we all dove for cover.

"Then who the hell is it, Chief?"

"Christ, Manta-Ray, I don't know! I just that it ain't my sister! Maybe it's some crazy fucker wearing a wig."

The chief's instincts were incredibly astute, as always. As the shooter at the barn spun around to run back inside, the wig fell off onto the gravel. It was a short, husky man in an old woman's dress who ran back into the dim lights, which were immediately extinguished.

Chief Bigelow had stopped, his mind had vacillated in one the shock of the moment, and he'd called me by my childhood nickname, Manta-Ray.

By the time our reinforcements made it up the hill and we'd found Mattie tied up in an outbuilding after searching the whole spread, we found out that the Robinsons were out of town, visiting relatives in Quillayute for a week, and Mattie couldn't tell us a thing – she'd been sitting in her living room, watching TV, when she felt a gun in the back of her neck and a cold, quiet voice told her not to resist as another unknown person blindfolded her from behind and they tied her up.

The reason for the impersonation was anybody's guess. We'd heard the imposter call us half-breeds – maybe it had to do with Mattie's Native American activism, or – maybe it was just a ploy to throw us off while they tried an assassination.

As for Spreckles – all we'd found was a blood trail heading into the woods – and, despite a statewide all-points and B.O.L.O., he'd never been seen or heard from again.

Until now.

Chapter 6

"Yeah, I've heard of Spreckles. I know who Spreckles is, as you damn well know. You're reading my criminal apprehension and charge book. I haven't heard that name mentioned for ten years, Opo. So, what the fuck's it all about?"

The warning look that Big Deb had given me started flashing in my mind like the neon sign of a cheap hotel – beware, keep out, don't stop here, giant cockroaches will be your bedmates.

Opo lit a cigar, took a puff.

"You know my sister lives on the Hood Canal."

"Nope, Ope, wasn't aware of that fact. If it is, in fact, a fact. You know what us cops used to say – never trust a fed."

Opo smirked, curling his lips around the cigar. He took it out and tapped ashes onto the deck.

"Yeah, well, she lives way out there, down around the Great Bend, up out of Tahuya – across the river and into the trees. You ever hear of the Martians?"

I'd heard of the Martians.

Up out of Tahuya, which was the site of an ancient fishing village, located where the Hood Canal takes a great bend and divides the Nooksak Peninsula from the Olympic mountains, the old DeWatto road links up with another remote, rural paved road called the Lost Highway. It was hard to find; there weren't any signs or turnoff lanes. In the daytime you'd miss it unless you were counting miles or knew the lay of the land and the forest; at night it didn't even exist unless you lived there.

The Lost Highway, after 15 miles or so, forked into several dirt roads which fueled into an enormous marsh. Out there in the tulies, people lived in trailers, old mobile homes, shacks, log cabins. To the locals, they were known as the Martians, being that they lived in a marsh, were rarely seen in any nearby towns (like Belfair, 50 miles away) and lived like aliens. Or – like the old Indians that some of them were.

"Yeah, I know about the Martians. I'm starting to get an inkling here, Opo. Spreckles has been spotted in Martian country, huh?"

"Not exactly. My sister plays on Sunday evenings at the Glow Room Tavern, in Belfair. She sits in with the band there, and since the drummer lives jus tdown the road from her in Tahuya, she rides in and back with me.

Opo watched Tom's face.

"He's a good guy, Tom, a carpenter who's making in on his own. And yeah, they see each other on the side. They both like to fish."

He eyed Tom closer. "You've only seen my sister play two songs, chatted with her for twenty minutes, and you feel protective of her, like she's your daughter, don't you?"

"Yep. I felt that way the first minute into her first song."

Opo smiled. "You're not the first wishful daddy she's had, buddy. And you won't be the last. Anyway, about 6 weeks ago, Nancy got in touch with me. She knows the old legend about Spreckles, and Mathilda, and Chief George Bigelow, of course. She's seen photos of Spreckles from back in the days when he was a tribal fish counter. And she's pretty sure that he comes into the Glow Room on Sunday nights, sits in the back at a table near the door, and watches her sing."

I felt my hackles rise up, like a badger, ready to deal with an animal digging at the door of his burrow.

"You remember the one of the fireworks places on the Suquamish Reservation, Cicuaci?"

"Yeah, sure. Those are my cousins on my mom's side."

"Right. Well, guess what. Georgie Jones is the drummer that gives Nancy rides to the Sunday gig. And guess what else – his uncle is Borkam Jones, the tribal cop who worked with you the night of the Pool Hills incident. The kid is positive the creep at the Glow Room watching him is Spreckles."

"So why didn't he go out and broach him? You know, ask him for a light, and make an ID? Kick his ass? What the fuck is this, Franklin? Unless Spreckles has committed a crime or is wanted on warrants, you've go no reason to run – "

I stopped. I looked inside my mind for clues. And I saw it.

"Why did you ask me about the Chacuici fireworks stand? That's the one out by the junction at the main highway – across from the big new casino. The feds want more control over reservation casinos – how many are built – and whether to start taxing gambling and fireworks sold on reservation land. You told me that Nancy stands to inherit – what – a couple million? Her Aunt Mathilda was an activist – she was against big casinos. The other tribal elders voted her down. Spreckles wasn't a visitor at the Pools Hills incident – he was a player. The ammo fired into him that me and Two-Horse saw – that was fake. Even those blood trails into the woods – he had some of his own blood to dribble on the ferns, as easily accessible as cutting his own hand. Somebody helped him get away, while we were busy searching the compound. The whole thin was a set-up, to make Mattie look bad, and to confuse this issue of the big casinos."

I paused.

"But the casinos have been good for the tribe – both of them – and environmental damage has been minimal."

"You're hitting on all the slot machines, Big Tom. Now move over to the big one – the one that takes ten-dollar bills, and spits out the big winner. You're almost there, buddy.

"It ain't the tribe, and it ain't the environment. It ain't the state tax commission, and it ain't the local government. Think about Nancy. Did she happen to mention that she and her band, Thistlebone, are up for a shot at playing in the big casino? Think about the couple of million bucks she stands to inherit. Think about the fact that she wants to follow in her Aunt Mattie's footprints, and use that money as a Native American activist working on Indian rights, education, and medical centers. And think about another thing – what Spreckles must be like, now. An assassin, funded by God knows who? A torture janitor? A killer of pretty, young, girl singers? We're not sure who's involved in this, Tom. But, one thing we've decided – you could be a big help. You and Big Deb."

Just then, Deb burst through the doors to the deck.

"Tom, I know everything he told you. He came earlier this afternoon and laid the whole thing out in my office. Honey – you're out of law enforcement! Two more good years with the bar and your music agency and we can retire! Tell him no, Big Tom. Tell him NO!"

Deb slid into the chair next to me, starting into my eyes, holding my hands. They call her Big Deb, and she is a big-boned, Swedish girl of old farm stock, but she can be very diminutive and feminine when she wants to be.

I had to decide. Really, it was a no-brainer, but I gave it another minute, as if I were thinking about it, so that Deb's explosion wouldn't be as – explosive.

"Deb, I've got to do it. I'm the only guy for the job – I know Spreckles, I can go undercover as a music agent for Nancy, and I can make moves with my old tribal connections. It's a natural, Deb. Besides, to tell you the truth honey," – I looked into her big brown, Swedish/Finnish eyes – "I've been a little bit bored, with the bar, and the music agency. This will be my last adventure – I promise. Besides – Opo Franklin there will protect me."

I looked over at Opo. "Right, partner?"

"Well…"

Deb exploded, just like I knew she would. "Find yourself an apartment, Big Asshole, and I'll talk to you in a few weeks – maybe!" She flounced back through the doors into the bar.

I looked at Opo. "What this 'well' shit, asshole? Are we partners in the field or not?"

Opo stubbed out his cigar, drained the last of his drink, and looked me in the eye. "You still got your service weapon?"

"Yeah, my old Ruger 38. Haven't cleaned it lately, though. It's wrapped up in a rag soaked in gun oil, in a box on the top shelf of my closet. Nowadays I carry this."

I pulled out the Glock nine millimeter out of my shoulder holster.

"It's not the one with the seventeen-round clip, only holds twelve. She'll do the job, though. I always carry an extra clip. Just in case I meet up with an asshole like you, who wants to blow holes in my life."

Opo stared me down. "I know you got a permit to carry, Tom. And I know that your law enforcement experience is extensive. But – I also know that you've never gone undercover before – playing one personality – the one you're known by, the one that is who you are – off another, no-less-believable personality, the one that you must now become. If these guys – our foes – these evil people – who you will come to see are as evil as anything on the planet – believe for a second that you are lying to them, and leading them on – it's not just you who will die, man. Big Deb, Nancy, Georgie, even myself – the guy talking to you now, dude – will be tortured and killed. And they'll make it happen. They'll make it happen in such a way that no one – not our friends, not our relatives, our tribal brothers, or the feds will know that it happened – it will, as they say in the movies, 'look like a natural accident'. Are you ready for that?"

"I don't like melodrama, but yeah – I'm ready. It takes a lot to scare Big Deb – and a lot for her to kick me out of the family bed. But you know you already had me, Opo. You also know that I'm gonna use up all my old-cop good ol' boy connections to check out you, Nancy, and everything you say. Other than that, where do we start?"

Chapter 7

"Right here," said Chief Myron George Bigelow, walking through the doors. "How's about another round, boys?"

Opo's eyes met mine. "Big Tom – I've got to leave, now. The chief will fill you in."

Opo got up, and after a moment's respectful hesitation, embraced the stocky, grey-haired eminence who stood next to him. With a nod to me, he left the deck through the gate in the fence and walked out into the parking lot – gone, as the lights glittered in the rain.

"Big Tom."

Chief Bigelow's eyes glistened, his eyebrows bounced, his nose twitched, his grin revealed old, stained teeth which had never been capped or replaced.

"I won't ask how you are, because I already know. I won't ask what you talked about with Franklin Opano – or Opo Frank, as we call him – because I already know. You see, he works for me. I will be your covert control, Agent Manta-Ray. Or how about, just Ray, for short. Your contact name for me will be Georgio. You like it? It fits in with the continental, European look we've been building into the lobbies of our new casinos."

The chief lowered his bulk into the chair that Opo had vacated, as two new drinks appeared – brought by a waitress who set them down quickly, cut a glance at Big Tom, and went back through the doors.

I settled back, and looked deep into old George's eyes. I'd known this guy for forty-five years, I thought. Haven't seen him for, how long? Since my son's commencement out of the police academy in Seattle, five years ago. And now, here he is, sitting before me, taking a sip of a double-rum cocktail, grinning like an old bear. I love him, like a father, or – an old, treasured uncle – but he's a wolf. Never forget that, baby.

He's an old wolf. And there's nothing that you have to be more careful of on this planet than an old wolf, looking across the table at you on the midnight deck of your own bar.

"Well, hello, Mr. Badger. You're in with the feds now, huh? I thought you got out of the cop game when you retired. And now – you say you're gonna be my cover officer? Shit, George. I'll tell you what – I'll meet you down on West Bay beach, and we can wrestle for the first day fishing rights. What was that – almost 50 years ago, pard. Now, don't be weirding me out like this."

Myron George Bigelow leaned forward, to fix his eyes on Tom, much as Franklin Opano had done earlier. But – this time, the eyes had much more force. They were the yellow/brown eyes, surrounded by Indian black, that carried the power and vigilance of centuries of tribal war and chiefdom. They carried the wisdom and pain of many decisions made of a tribal elder, under pressure from forces that predated modern corporations.

"I speak now, Tom Mooney, to a respected warrior of the Suquamish Tribe. Your mother, Chin-coot.nai, was loved and revered, as were her ancestors, as are her children.

"However, Manta-Ray – we do have a problem, which it seems, only you and I, myself, are uniquely qualified to address."

"Yeah, I know, Spreckles. I remember the whole Pool-Hills thing like it was yesterday, Chief. And I understand why I'm involved. I'll go into the field tomorrow, OK? I've still got connections. We'll find this guy."

Chief Bigelow leaned back in his chair. "Tom, when was the last time you talked to your son?"

My son, Jaimie, born 27 years ago, was now an active remodeling contractor in Nipsak County, as well as a reserve Nipsak County deputy sheriff. Since Big Deb, his mother, was one-half Swedish and one-half Finnish, and I, his father, was one-half Irish and one-half American Indian – mostly of the Suquamish Tribe – we'd argued for many hours over what to name him.

In the end, we compromised. James Chiquici George Pekonen Mooney was the names he became, to befit a child of Swedish, Finnish, Native Indian Irish stock. And so – Jaimie he became known as.

"Why? Why, George – what's my son got to do with this?"

"Tom, Nancy broke up with that drummer. They're still friends, and everything is cool between them. Now, she's seeing Jaimie."

"What? Jesus, George. There's too many fucking coincidences here, too many tribal connections! I just saw this girl play her music tonight for the first time – I'd never seen, or heard of her before! And now, in the last 2 hours, I'm hit with stuff that has to do with our old police work, on a case involving a missing asshole that nobody even heard about for years, and you're saying my son, Jaimie, is involved? What the fuck – I told Franklin I'd work on this thing. I told Deb – and now's she's pissed. She tried to warn me. Goddammit – like I told Opo – never trust a fed. And you're a fed – aren't you, George?"

Chief Bigelow looked sad and concerned. He nodded assent.

"And now you say my son is involved? How?"

"Well, actually, Manta-Ray – Jaimie is the link, the key to our investigation. You see, when our girl Thistlebone – excuse me, I mean Nancy – first called Franklin, she told him that she'd already talked to your son about seeing Spreckles at her gig in the Glow Room."

"Well, shit. How the hell did they know each other?"

Jaimie Mooney first met Nancy in the local Belfair grocery store. He'd been following her around since he'd first spotted her in the dairy aisle – and had then followed her discretely, pushing his shopping cart, tossing items in at random as she moved her cart through the canned food aisles, the produce section, and the butcher counter – where she asked for one pound of Italian sausage and one pound of salmon – he caught up with her there.

"Why are you buying salmon at the butcher shop in a store?" he asked.

She looked over at him, shook out her auburn hair, disdainfully, and answered – "Because I want to. Why are you asking?"

Jaimie reared his head back, about 4 inches, and regrouped. He had no idea what to say.

"Because, I know where to get better salmon. I mean, I can get fresh Chinook –"

"But only Indians can do that now, on Hood Canal. Are you Indian?"

"Yes."

"But I like to shop here, and I don't like to buy from those Skokomish assholes down around Great Bend. I know it's fresher, and I know that they think I'm a mean bitch. But they always hit on me."

She regarded him. "Are you hitting on me?"

"Yes."

The butcher came forward, and pushed her order over the counter. "Thank you, ma'am. Have a nice day."

Nancy took her wrapped package of fish and put it in her cart.

"Don't you hate it, when they say that 'nice day' shit? Don't you want to tell them where to stick it?" asked Jaimie.

"What's your name, you uppity fool?"

"Jaimie. What's yours?"

"Nancy. Now – will you leave me alone, before I call security?"

"Nancy? Nancy! Nobody is named Nancy anymore. My god – the last time I heard of a girl named Nancy was, well – never! I've heard of it, in the past, probably back in my mom and dad's time, but no girl now is named –"

"I know, I know, stupido. I've heard it all before. I'm the last of the Nancies. Now – will you please go away and let me shop?"

"Wait. Here, let me show you something. You see this can of pineapples in my cart?"

Nancy looked into Jaimie's cart. She saw a can of pineapple chunks. She looked up into his inquiring face. "Yeah? So what?"

"Well, Nancy. Over in the next aisle, we have the wine and beer aisle."

"So?"

"So, I know how to make this really great dish – first I barbecue the salmon, with lemon, garlic, and thyme. Then I miss the canned pineapple chunks up with white wine, tomatoes, garlic, and zucchini, which I dump into a large frying pan with olive oil. It's cooking on low. Then I pull the salmon off the grill and dump the zucchini mix over the fish – what? Doesn't that sound good? Why are you looking at me like that?"

"Well, it does sound good. Are you asking me to dinner?"

"Yes, I am. But – I won't use salmon that has been aging behind the counters of this butcher shop. We need fresh fish. You know?"

"OK, then. That rules out tonight."

"Huh?"

"That rules out tonight, you idiot. Unless you've just caught some, and it's sitting in the back of your truck, stinking and going bad, or unless you're gonna run out right now and go catch some – huh? You gonna do that? No, I don't think so. Well, then. Tonight's off. Maybe some other time."

Nancy gave him her dimpled smile, and started pushing her cart away.

"Wait, wait – wait a minute, will you?"

Jaimie jammed his cart up next to hers. "Will you just wait, for a second? Here – let me give you my card." He pulled out his wallet, fished around inside, and came up with a wrinkled business card, which he delivered to her with a flourish. She sighed, shifted her weight to her left foot, then her right. She looked at him with extremely dubious eyes.

"Well, what's this. A business card. How original." She did take it out of his hand, however, and looked it over. His hopes soared. "Jaimie Mooney, remodeling – all phases," she read aloud. Her voice carried inflections of sarcasm and scorn. "Includes tile, drywall, small additions, and decks. Why 'small' additions? You can't handle large ones?"

"Oh, sure, as a matter of fact, we just put a bid down on a 1,400 square foot master bedroom suite, just outside of Fragaria Ridge."

"I'll keep the card –" she squinted at it again – "Jaimie. Don't call us, we'll call you." She started to move her cart away.

"Wait! I mean, can you just hang on for a second? Look – I feel something here. Don't you? I don't see no wedding ring – I mean, uh – excuse me – I hadn't noticed a ring on your wedding hand, I mean, uh, are you single? Would you like to have dinner down on the beach sometime? I've got a place on the water –we can pick up oysters and put them on the grill right there, on the beach in front of my deck. The way I cook oysters is…"

"I like my oysters raw, cowboy." Nancy cut her eyes at him, and swiveled her hips. "But – you seem OK to me. Shy and stupid, but with a good energy. So - I'll tell you what. I'll give you my number at work – I work part time down at the Suquamish Center. When you call, patch through to extension 117. But – listen – don't leave any weird message. I've been getting some of those lately. And yes, I am single at the moment – not to get your hopes up, stupido. Now, go catch some salmon." Nancy handed Jaimie her business card. "See?" she pointed at the voicemail number, with its extension. "No weird messages. We'll be taping you. If you leave a weird message, we'll have the cops at your door."

Jaimie chuckled. "Now, that's ironic. The cops at my door…"

"What's ironic about it? I'm not kidding!"

"Oh, no, nothing, um, um, um, Nancy. Nothing. I'm in good with the cops."

She eyed him again, intensely.

"Yeah, uh huh. OK, cowboy. Go on your merry way, OK? Not another word, or I'll yell for security."

"OK, Nancy. No need to freak out. I'll, uh, go my merry way. You gonna call me? And by the way – there's no security cops ijn this store. Why do you keep saying that?"

"I have a pet dragon in my purse." She patted the leather bag sitting in her shopping cart. "He comes when I call."

"Well, so will I, you sweetheart. So will I."

Her cheeks colored, and after a second, so did his.

"I mean, um, I didn't mean nothin'…"

"It's OK. That's one of the coolest things you've said yet. I just might – look – I'll call you tomorrow, OK? I can tell you're part Indian – but you look like a cowboy to me. We'll have to get you a cowboy hat." She dimpled again, as she moved away. "See you later, alligator."

With one last challenging look over her shoulder, Nancy walked away, pushing her shopping cart. Jaimie stood rooted to the spot for 3 ½ minutes. Then he turned and walked over to the butcher counter.

"Can I help you, sir?" asked the counter man.

"Yeah. Tell me how to figure out women."

The butcher laughed. "Oh, that's easy. Take everything you know, divide it by 12, subtract 10, and use the sum of the result to measure the number of stars in the sky."

Chapter 8

Outside, many miles away, in one of the myriad inlets and saltwater-filled valleys of the great Salish Sea, otherwise known as Puget Sound, a small motor-sailer changed course to follow the incoming tide as a brace of bald eagles wrestled overhead and the first lambent rays of the setting sun serrated their way across the sky. It was a ferryboat in miniature, a tiny tame ferry that Spreckles rode, heading up Dewatto Bay into the cut – a slice of light that had narrowed to almost closing.

But – it was still there, to those who knew where to go. He cut the motor and rigged sail, which luffed, luffed again, then ballooned in the evening breeze as he pulled the rudder to slide the skiff across the current. He was following his blood – which ran with the tide – and so was feeling his way in tune with the same natural forces he knew from so many years ago. He'd only come this way before by boat – and so it was the way he was returning. Lifting his face, his gauge lofted up towards the majestic Olympic mountains. As near as a few beats of a soaring eagle's wing, as far as many hours of rugged hiking, - green as a verdant jungle on a the lower slopes, with clear-cut logging patches here and there – all the way up to the glaciers, still sleeping amongst the verdant heights as the trees turned to enormous boulder fields and the eagles flew over a high-mountain coulee, out of sight.

But, not out of his heart. He was with them, inescapably. Their journey was his journey, now that he'd chosen to return – back to the ancient nest.

A song came into his mind, as his heart stayed with the hidden wings of the eagles.

"A cool wind
blew through
and stopped us

before we could start
but now
after you
I look
up
at the moon
as the clouds
break apart
and I know
that we
are together
again
Just like the
eagles
whose wings
fly on the wind."
Spreckles, although that is not now, and never was, his name, turns his eye back to the hissing waters under his bow and begins to reel his boat toward the shore of a hidden cove.

Chapter 9

As the applause died down, Nancy stepped back up to the micro-phone. She nodded to the bass player, who was holding up two fingers.

"Well, thanks, folks. Everybody feeling ok?"

The roar of 5,000 voices answered her in the affirmative.

"Well, alright then. We've just got a couple more tunes to go, so here's something a little more rough house for ya. I'm gonna get some help here with some back up singers. You all know 'em, I think – it's Jim, Bob, and Tina, from the Nomads!"

Another roar from the crowd as the band now known as "Thistle-bone" swung into one of their up and coming hits, "That's How It Goes".

"You came home stinking
said you didn't get the job
and then you got kidnapped
by an angry mob.
You said they took you by force
Out to a strange golf course
And made you admit that after all, you're just slob.
Oh, but darlin', I forgive you
'cause that's just how it goes.
First they take your money
and then they take your clothes.
If you can't even trust
The ones that you think you know
Then the ones that you don't
Will show you just how far away it goes.
You said what about
all the good things that I did.
I dug ditches in the rain

and I raised two lovely kids.
Now one of them's in jail
and the other's on the run
but I swear it wasn't because
of anything that I have done.
And I said darlin',
that's just how it goes.
First they take your money
and then they take your clothes.
Before you even know it
they'll steal everything, you know.
And we say, my God, I've been robbed!
but baby, baby baby, that's just the way it goes.

The lights caromed across the stage, as Nancy and her band raised their arms together in a tribute to the crowd.

"You guys have been great! We love you! Now, we've got to go, darlin's – we've got a hot date down in Tennessee!"

The band backed away from the microphones as they linked hands and raised their arms together one last time.

"Bye!" shouted Nancy. "We love you!"

They dropped arms and walked towards the back of the stage, past one drum kit into the netherworld behind the curtains. The screams and yells for more subsided into the background as they went down the staircase and into a tunnel-like hallway to the backstage dressing rooms.

"Aye, we nailed 'em to the wall tonight, mates," exulted Roger, the Australian drummer. "Shit, this is almost the funnest band I've toured with – except maybe the 'Large Rat and Gopher Society'."

Nancy let out a huge woosh and fell onto one of the sofas. "Damn, you guys, I'm bushed," she woofed.

"You sure are, baby," pronounced Tow Truck, the bass player, nudging her ankle with his boot. "I swear, your panties are bulging – you can see it through your skirt. Want me to give you a pube trim, special tongue rate?"

"Shut up, assbrain," she replied. "I got all the action I need with Little Rick and his roadies. Huh, Rick?"

Little Rick loomed up from behind a dressing table. "Yup. Back down your fizz, fuck ball," he intoned.

"Hey, man, no worries," said Tow Truck. "I was just funnin', is all. It was a towering great gig tonight, in case you didn't notice. Just givin' our gal a little whirl." He grinned, winked at Nancy, and licked his lips.

"Just glad you mates picked me up on this tour, I was fookin' bleedin' me heart to death, waitin' in that hotel in Albuquerque – what a fookin' hell hole, eh, Champus?"

"Jesus Christ – quit trying to sound like Roger," A.J. "Champ" Calhoun looked up with sleep-riddled eyes, bored out of his skull with the same old backstage after-show banter he'd heard so many thousands of times. And nobody was doing drugs anymore to blank out the pain. Now it was all health food crackers, bowls of fruit, and imported water with fancy labels, to make you think you were drinking champagne. "Yeah, yeah, right, you big doofus. Call me when you got something original to say."

He crossed his blue jeans, and sunk deeper into the couch. "One thing, Nancy – look at this on the video playback when you start the second chorus of 'Blue Belle', you look around at Leonard like you're gonna strangle him."

"That's because he missed the block chord sustain," she hissed, glaring at her keyboard player. "He's supposed to bring that cascade down just before, not after I start singing…"

Nancy's cell phone blurted out the "Star Spangled Banner" lead guitar by Jimi Hendrix from Woodstock.

"Now, I wonder who that could be?" rang out numerous humorous voices.

"Yeah, yeah, you geeks, I'm sure it's Cowboy. I am married, you know." She flipped open the phone, tossing aside her long auburn hair, and putting it to her ear. "Hey, Pig," she said with a glowing smile.

"Hey, Piglet. How'd it go?"

"Oh, baby, we've got Cleveland in the palm of our hand. Next stop, Tennessee."

"Yeah, how many shows there?"

"Three – Chattanooga, Memphis, and Nashville – Tom said he'd meet us there, for the last show on the tour. With all the label guys and promos. And – get this, Pig – it might be on live TV. Tom said the governor loves our music, and he might be there too, and you're gonna be there, right?"

"Piglet."

"Yeah?"

"I don't know if I can make it. Probably Tom can't, either."

Nancy's eyes went into a concentrated slant as she bounced up off the couch and walked away into a corner, away from her noisy band mates. "What's going on, Cowboy? Is it a cop thing?"

"Yeah, Nance, it is. It involves tribes, and it involves you, too, Piglet. I can't say too much right now – here, say hello to your baby girl."

"Hoquiam? What's she doing up at this hour?"

"Well, I put her down after dinner, and I was doing the crossword puzzle when she crawled into my lap just before I called you."

"You fell asleep in the recliner with her – didn't you? I'm not mad. Just don't snap that thing forward so fast that she falls off onto the floor…"

There was a tiny female gurgle over the phone, and then a screech.

"Hey, baby girl! Your mommy did good tonight, darlin' – they was screamin'! They loved us better than honey buttered hotcakes! Who's my girl, huh? Who's my baby girl? Ho, ho, Hoquiam, that's who! Yeah!"

The gurgles and screeches almost blew out Nancy's eardrum – she held the phone away and eyed it with a loving, brown-eyed squint. "Honey, honey, put the big pig back on the line – Cowboy? You there?"

"Yeah, Piglet. She just pooped her pannies. Hang on a minute." There was a rustling sound, and the screeches subsided back down to happy gurgles. "She's okay for a minute. I'm standing up now, and she's over my shoulder. Oops – she just puked – and now here comes Mr. Bones to lap it up." Mr. Bones was their old yellow Labrador. "Anyway, Nance – Tom will be talking to you tomorrow to give you a heads-up on this shit – I've gotta go change the baby, hon. Love ya – bye."

"Pig! Cowboy! Wait a minute! You there?" She was holding a dead phone.

Chapter 10

As the green and white slab of a state ferryboat lit up like a sparkling emerald and moved north towards the San Juan Islands, an eagle cut loose with its keening cry in the heavy evening air. Lummi Island, far to the north in the Salish Sea, a pow-wow of sorts was being conducted deep in the woods, off the back roads – the only kind of roads that existed there, at least until the McWhite tribe started building their McMansions. Then, huge panel driveways disappeared into old native lands behind dark, forbidding gates. The McWhites had taken what they could, and built where they could. But – that was pretty much over, now.

A few of the local tribal elders were gathered, along with a medicine woman and an interloper from an outside past, who was attempting to claim certain rights, or at least advice he might get. And so the meeting had been called.

"Chuik In-des-ka, you say that you want us to monitor an investigation into incidents that happened in your past, when you were growing up as a member of another tribe, one Suquamish, to the south of us. Yet, you say you will not speak until you are told that we hold our involvement secret, and that you are still a vested member of that tribe, having not been shunned or ousted. Is that about it?"

"Yes, Elder Charlie. And, I seek the advice of your clan of Elders, also."

"Why our clan in particular? Why don't you seek the wisdom and guidance of your own elders, who know of you and your life-spirit? Have you traveled so far off your given path? Are you a warrior, in truth, or possibly a criminal, or a drug addict? We get a lot of those, you know. We usually make a few calls and bust them back to their own soil, to face the music."

"No, Elder Charlie. I have done some bad things in the past, but it's nothing worse than is common for a stupid youth with mixed-up blood – or pure blood, for that matter. No, this thing I want to speak to the council about involves many of my own tribal members, and goes far beyond the boundaries of our reservation."

"Then, tell us also, Chuik In-des-ka, what other tribes know of these things in the past, and why we should hold what you might tell us now secret from them? After you tell us that, we will decide whether or not we want anything to do with it. Right, Elder Sam?"

"Right, Onreeska-Se. But, having said this, let's see what this man of Suquamish has to say. He is not a puppy, yet in his full-grown dog-hood, he still may have an interesting tail. He is able to face us, eye-to-eye, and so we will treat with him, assuming he has held on to his honor as a man – and not just a dog."

There was a pregnant silence, as they sat around the woodstove, and the fire crackled.

"Hey, Larry?"

"Yeah."

"Not to interrupt anything, but I'm an old woman and my arthritis is acting up. Can we get this thing done, whatever it is? I want to go home and watch TV."

"Chuik In-des-ka, this is Walking-Feather, a wise woman who agreed to join us to…"

"Cut the shit, Larry. Everybody knows that you're a gabber; you'll gab all this traditional shit until the chickens come home." She faced the one who was known as Spreckles. "Listen, you. I know who you are. I go way back with some of your people in Suquamish. I don't have anything against you – and I know a lot more about this stuff you're talking about than anybody else in this room. And they don't have anything against you either. That guy there – he's a plumber. That guy over there, hiding against the wall – he makes his living at the casino, walking around like he knows something. OK. So, everything else aside, they called me in here tonight because they know that I know something about you, and because they know I wouldn't take any shit. Also, keep in mind that if you lie to us, about anything – we'll know.

Lummi Indians are good at that. So – let's hear what you've got to say before old Larry over there goes more traditional on us and pukes his guts out. OK?"

"OK." Chiuk started to talk.

Chapter 11

Cowboy saw his old Subaru wagon with the cream-colored Mo-Joc rims in the parking lot of the state liquor store. He'd sold it to Al's Country Auto the winter before, when he'd had two other cars, plus one one-ton van, his driveway packed with vehicles. So he'd driven down to Al's, past the Bethel-Burley crossroads, on a freezing day of light falling snow. Al was from the old school; even smoked a cigar.

"I'll give ya a hundred bucks. Ya got the title?"

"Al, this is a four-wheel drive Subaru wagon, an '86. Look, the body is clean, just a crack or two in the windshield, I admit it needs a wheel bearing, but it runs good and…"

"It needs a hell of a lot more than that. It needs to get off my lot. See ya."

"OK - $150, but only because I'm short of dough. You're killing me."

"Yeah sure, cowboy, come inside, get warm, and I'll write you a check. Hey – how are you gonna get back home?"

Now, this winter, two years later, going to the state liquor store anyway, so he followed the Sube in and parked nearby. It looked pretty much the same – right down to the half-roll of electrical tape he'd used to hold the right side mirror on – new windshield, though. Nice.

He noticed a pang of remorse, or perhaps regret – anyway, one of those "R" words – went through him. The car looked better than he'd remembered it – the body really was straight, and a cool magenta color that went excellent with the Mo-Jocs. He walked carefully around it, noticing a pudgy lady lying back in the passenger side. Oh yeah, the seats reclined – and were plush velour. Shit. Why had he even sold it?

He went inside and grabbed his usual bottle of Bailey's Irish Cream. He saw the guy who'd gotten out of the Subaru, next in line.

"Hey – did you get that Subaru down at Al's Auto?"

The guy looked at him, suspicious. "Yeah, why?"

"I used to own it. I drove that thing for five years, man."

The guy brightened up. "Cool."

"Still runs good, huh?"

"Yeah, great. I drive it to Auburn every day."

"Damn, that's a ways. Mind if I ask what you paid Al for it?"

"Eight hundred. But I had to put in a right rear strut, and a new windshield."

"Huh. I'll be damned."

The guy got rung up, nodded, and walked out the door.

After Cowboy had sold it to Al, the Sube had disappeared from view – he knew Al's son was working on it. Then, that summer, all shined up, it appeared on the lot with an American flag flying on its antenna, and Cowboy almost shit when he saw the price Al had on it - $1450. All summer long, he'd driven by there, on the road out of town to his place, laughing like a hyena. He's crazy! He'll never come close to that. What's he thinking? Maybe $650 with a new windshield.

But, it still looked good. It was a cool-looking car. And the liquid glass he'd applied in to the engine had seemed to seal the blown head gasket. Hell, he'd driven it for two years after that. That glass stuff worked.

And now, from behind the wheel of his Nissan truck, he pulled out of the state liquor lot around the corner to a stop sign. Across the four-way, another car waved through. It was a yellow '89 Subaru wagon, driven smartly by an old lady with spectacles.

"I'll be damned," thought Cowboy. He took a left into the Safeway Mall, almost running into a white '89 Subaru wagon chugging out of a parking space the wrong way with a fat, crazy-looking Indian inside.

"No – shit. You've got to be kidding me."

Once out of the store, crossing the lot toward his truck, here came a black '85 Subaru wagon, running well, but with a possible busted shackle.

"Holy crap…"

On the way home, he saw two more, for a total of five seen in the hour or so since he'd seen his old one at the state liquor store. CAR MAGIC. CAR SORCERY.

You never notice a certain kind of car until you buy one, and start driving it around. Or – sell one. Then you see them everywhere you go.

But this – this was something else. This was five in one hour, of something he'd sold. This was car sorcery in reverse.

He went home, got up on his deck, and poured a double Bailey's over ice. I don't think I'll leave the house for a while, he thought. Maybe they'll all go away.

One night in Seattle, down in Pioneer Square in the early eighties, he'd been drunk enough to see double and went running across Yesler Way onto First Avenue, then fell flat on his face. Seconds earlier, the light had changed, and twenty-five cars had rolled forward over the street where he now lay on his belly, clutching his eagle feather necklace, having tripped over the curb and fallen headlong. He got up on his scraped and bloody elbows and knees, and then finally stood, to the cheers of a few bums and other late-night revelers emptying out of bars.

"Hey, buddy – you almost got squished, asshole." A woman's laughter sounded like brittle china plates breaking on tile floor.

He clutched his eagle feather in his hand. It had saved him, he knew. That – and car magic. He'd fallen in the only space between heavy, cruising, Friday night traffic. He limped to the sidewalk, and flagged down a cab. It was only five blocks down to the ferry dock – but he wasn't taking any more chances, especially with the dark alleys that opened up onto Yelser Way.

You don't mess with Car Magic.

And now, here came Tom Mooney, driving the old clunker Cadillac Cowboy's mother used to own, spewing black smoke and backfiring all the way into his driveway. His dad leaned out the window, beaming, as the engine racked itself with paroxysms of post ignition and evil knocking noises.

"Hey, son! Remember when Big Deb used to drive this thing, after I finally taught her how? Man, she'd cruise down the streets like the Queen of Sheba, waving to all her friends…"

"She was usually drunk, Dad, remember? And it was you who finally pulled off the distributor cap and yanked the rotor when she was still inside the 'Sunny Side Up', having one too many with those so-called friends, those hambone, old broads."

"Yeah! Hey, that's right. You've got a good memory, son. You were there that night with me, out in the parking lot, huh? Man, how she bitched when this old fucker wouldn't start."

Cowboy rolled his eyes. "Yeah. Just like with you, later, in bed, huh? I bet some of them old gals got an earful about your dirty shenanigans..."

"Yeah, well, some of 'em know first-hand, so to speak."

As Big Tom heaved himself out of the old boat, the car door let out a horrendous shriek. "Jesus, that gave me the willies." He shuddered. "Sounded just like your mother, calling me to bed. Sometimes I'd just crawl out the window and walk down the back way to the bar..."

"Alright, Dad, that's enough. Let's go in the garage – I've got smoked salmon and some cold ones socked away in the little fridge."

"I'll be damned. You still got that thing? I remember when you stole that from me back when you were in Olympic College, just feeling your oats..."

"You gave it to me, Pop. Come on – I'll re-introduce you. It still works."

They walked together up towards the back of Cowboys' property, boots crunching on gravel as the mosquitoes sang and the owls hooted in the trees. A half moon was looming down through the second-growth firs and a night bird chimed like a bell.

"Hear that? That's a whippoorwill – looking for its mate."

Yeah, maybe. Or a landlord looking for his rent."

"Damn, boy, what the hell's the matter with you? You're as cynical as a dental hygienist."

"Yep. Parenthood will do that to you."

They trooped up through the shop into Cowboy's "Crows Nest" – a tiny room filled with rusted car parts, old guitars, faded pictures and the sweet tang of ancient grease. A getaway hole, the only window was blacked out with insulation and an old army blanket. Huge brown woodland moths skittered around a battery-powered Coleman lantern.

They settled into two dusty recliners as Cowboy leaned back, reached out with his boot, and slammed the door shut. Big Tom raised his eyebrows.

"What about Hoquiam? She in the main house?"

Cowboy pointed to a bundle, slumbering in a sweet, well-wrapped corner. "We ran around like a couple of hyenas earlier. She's down for a while. We played her favorite game out on the lawn behind the house."

"What favorite game?"

"Chasing farts. You know, I'd put out my finger, she'd pull it, I'd fart, then shed chase me around the yard until she caught me and we did it again."

"Yeah, I know, you turd. I taught it to you."

"Yeah, but you stunk up the whole yard, the neighbors complained, and Mom made us stop…"

"Okay, okay. Give me some of that smoked salmon, big shot."

As they chewed the red-brown, smoky goodness, the new-cop reserve son eyed the old cop retired father.

"So what's it about, Pop? Nancy is on the wing, she's got possible hit songs climbing the charts, and we can't meet her in Nashville? And what's this federal shit? Sounds to me like…"

"Well, Ke-ah-dah-le, as a matter of fact…"

"Wait, wait a minute. Indian names? We're gonna use our Indian names? Shit, I can't even remember yours."

"Bullshit."

"Oh yeah, that's it."

"When are you gonna cut the crap, Nooksak?"

"As soon as you do, Bullshit."

They both leaned back and sighed, then listened and leaned forward in unison as the baby murmured in her sleep and rustled in her cradle, then subsided.

Suddenly they were whispering.

"You think we woke her up?"

"Nah. She's cool. You know we can't smoke up here, though."

"Right. Let's grab another beer and go outside."

Tom leaned toward the tiny refrigerator, then stopped. Cowboy was eying him with heavy, downcast brows.

"What?"

"I was making a joke, Mr. Bullshit. Are you telling me you still…"

"Yeah, yeah. Only you could bait a trap like that, canoodling your old man. Seems to me I see a pack of Marlboros sitting over there behind the Army blanket…"

"OK, let's go."

"What about the baby?"

Cowboy patted his shirt pocket. "I got a two-way radio right here, Pop. A baby monitor. They didn't have them when you had us. We just had to yell if no one was around."

Tom got up and looked into the crib. Sure enough, a plastic box with soft, rounded edges was clipped to the edge of the cradle, a green light blinking.

"I can turn it up while we're outside, and the sound of her breathing will shake the owls out of the trees. Speaking of owls."

"What?"

"I'll tell you outside. C'mon – let's go. Grab a couple beers. Quiet, now."

They grooked out of their recliners and tiptoed through the shop.

Outside, under the huge, random night, forested by the green umbrella, Tom whispered.

"Hey, this is great, son. No one around to yell at us."

"We can talk normal, Dad. The nearest neighbor is old Bob Hedges, and he went deaf years ago. Besides – I don't think it's so great. I wish Nancy was here. I wish my girl was home, and not on the road. It's starting to bug me – really bug me."

Cowboy took a pull off his cigarette as Big Tom contemplated him.

"You know, in the beginning, when I started managing her, I knew she'd go places fast. But what I didn't know was that you and her even knew each other, much less…"

"I know, man. I know. You were just doing your job, your gig. And you did it well. If it wasn't you, it would have been somebody else. Nancy wasn't gonna be held down, no way. We all knew she'd be busting out of Podunksville."

"Okay. So what's this shit about owls?"

"Well, the other night I got up to pee, checked the baby, and went into the kitchen. It was about 5 a.m. You know that big window by Mom's old desk – I've got it screened for the summer, and it was wide open. I was thinking about a beer – decided not to."

"Well, that's good. Jesus."

"Yeah. Well, you know, I miss Nancy. Anyway, I sat down and started writing."

"Writing what?"

"I'll tell you about it later. Anyway, I was deep in a blue funk and it was quiet as hell. It was so quiet, I didn't even know how quiet it was – the absence of any sound at all, the whole forest asleep, had put me asleep, even though I was awake. You know what I mean?"

"Yeah. Yeah, I know. Go on."

Cowboy paused, field stripped his cigarette, obviously troubled. His brow got crooked like a wrinkled sock.

"Well, I'll tell you man, suddenly there was this sound – from deep in the woods, outside the kitchen window – it was like the woods themselves, the trees were talking; but it wasn't just the trees. It nearly blew me out of my chair."

"It was spirits – ancient woodland spirits."

"Yeah, shit, whatever – it was like, old voices. At first, as I started listening, waking up out of my trance, I thought it was random – like maybe just a couple of owls, you know. But – then – I realized it was a conversation. It was a fucking conversation, and there was nothing human about it. I was scared shitless."

"What did you do?"

"I grabbed a flashlight and went out there – what do you think I did?"

"What did you see out there?"

"Well, I left the flashlight on the deck, started to walk into the trees – then I thought of the baby, and ran back to the house. But, that ain't all."

"What else?"

"The other night I was driving the back roads, coming home from Seattle after doing a tile job at a restaurant over in Lynwood. I had to work at night, after they closed. It was, like five in the morning again."

"What about Hoquiam?"

"She was at Molly's, spent the night there."

"Okay."

"Anyway, I'm going down Tracy Street…"

"Tracy, that little street back up behind your old apartment?"

"Yeah, and another owl, a big, white owl, flies out of a thistle thicket and hits the side of my truck hard, man! But I didn't know it was an owl, yet, okay? All I knew was this thing thumped into the side of my truck out of the darkness… so I stopped and got out, and here's this huge white owl…"

"White? He was all white?"

"Yeah, Dad, I'm not kidding – and he's standing in the road, feathers all around, one wing held out, straight from his side, like he was pointing at something, or warning me about something…"

"He hoot at you?"

"No, but he was looking straight at me. I said – shit, man, are you OK? And then he flew off into the bushes, underneath a tree, and then off into the sky – shit, man, he was huge…"

Suddenly, the baby monitor squawked.

"Uh, oh, Nooksak. It's your kid."

"No shit, Pop. She probably pooped her pannies. Let's go in."

"Hey, Nookie?"

"What?"

"There's something heavy going down, and the feds are involved. Also, old tribal shit."

"What is it, Pop?"

"I can't tell you now, son, it would take an hour. Let's go in, see about Hoquiam."

"OK – but what's the code on this shit, man?"

"Code is stand by, stand ready. I'll call you tomorrow."

"Alright – and I'll tell you about the other three owls."

"What?"

"Yeah, five in twenty-four hours."

"Damn."

"Yeah. Then I'll tell you about the five Subaru wagons."

"Wait a minute – what?"

Chapter 12

Little Hoquiam dreams of soft brown, corduroy shirtsleeves, the smoky-woodsy smell of the wonderful father who holds her, distant circular lights, floating globes of red, yellow, blue, and green, and windows in the dark, opening to soft voices on the other side of the screens; giant woodland moths with brown wings and yellow eyes, and an amorphous, ominous warning with rings like a distant bell. She is not worried, since 16-month old girls don't worry when they're loved, cared for, and wrapped in an Indian blanket. She will not remember these dreams, only as the night moths fly they fly through her sleeping mind. She breathes, and her eyelids flutter. Breathing, she smiles, wrinkles her brow, then frowns, and lets out a squall.

The voices, which had vanished to the edge of hearing, return. She smiles again – good, familiar smells are back, along with the soft, brown corduroy sleeves. The lights bounce and falter, then suddenly glow bright after a metallic screeching sound ends in a slam and thud. A car engine growls to life, then rattles away, reversing out of hearing. Then her father's voice – "Let's get you inside, Peanut. Time for all of us to be in bed. You too, Bonesy. Let's go, dog."

Hoquiam snuggles into the warm father arms as the sudden chill night air smells of forest. Then, the door, the carpet, the bed, the pillow. She smells Bones and hears him sigh as the lights go out and he lays down at the foot of her bed.

She knows no more, after her father's kiss. The door shuts quietly, the monitor glows green in the dark. She knows no more.

Chapter 13

Inside the plywood and tarpaper shack, sided with old cedar siding for camouflage, Mad Willie tended his chemicals and took another hit off the White Rhino – finest in the Northwest. Outside, the steady rain continued.

"Listen, motherfucker. I don't give a shit about what Yates says. We gonna make this drug my way, or we gonna shit-can the lab. We've gotta get this shit cooked down to a second mash by sunrise. Then we go to sleep – get up at 4:30, and have the third crush in the pan by midnight – or at least 2 a.m. I figure 20 ounces this batch. You with me, Turnip?"

Mad Willie turned his huge, pumpkin-like head towards his cohort, who resembled a similar vegetable – having a white, scrawny, hairy neck topped by diamond eyes in a head shaped like a triangle covered with greenish hair. He was dressed in a mini-skirt, high heels, and a silver sleeveless t-shirt. An unconscious girl had her head in his lap. She looked to be about fifteen.

"Listen, Will. I'm just a user, not a cooker, man. I don't know shit about this guy Yates. I just wanna help out around the lab, and dress up with the little girls, and get it on, you know?"

"Well, that's all well and good, Turnip. But we've got a fuckin' mission here. And neither you, nor Yates, nor little Ida there, nor Scooge, is gonna fuck this up. 'Cause we stand to make a lotta money here – you understand me, dickhead?"

The interior of the lab seemed to grow dim, as if a stroke of a lightening bolt had reversed itself, and the negative side of an ancient photograph had suddenly come to life.

Little Ida stirred in Turnip's lap, came awake, and yawned with an innocence completely out of place. She opened her eyes, stirred, stretched her arms, sat up, and looked around the room. "Hey, you guys – where's all the music?"

"Shit, Turnip," muttered Mad Willie. "That crap you gave her is wearing off – you didn't give her enough. You better dose her again before she starts sussing us out."

"Ok, ok. Hey, little wonder, I made you another drink. You liked the last one, didn't you?"

"Oh, yeah, Mr. Turnip. Hey, why you got that funny name? I mean, the drugs are cool and all, but I really should be getting on back to the party in the old fishing warehouse – you know, they're waiting for me back down there."

Mad Willie glared at Turnip with undisguised fury. "Who the fuck is she talking about? Who the fuck knows about us from the old fish warehouse? Why the fuck did you tell…"

"Hey, hey, hey," intoned a quiet, level voice. "Don't sweat, don't fret, ol' Johnny boy."

Into the room walked a regal figure, dressed in pink, green, and silver, similar to Turnip. He swiveled his head toward her and smiled in relief. She was a tall woman, standing in a relaxed mixture of serious insanity, one hand poised on a robust hip, the other passing a dark cigarette to her mouth. She took a slow puff, exhaled, and let out a disarming chuckle.

"You guys are getting paranoid, you know. I've got it under control down there at the old fish warehouse. Just keep cooking up the frac, freak. If everybody keeps his cool – we'll all be cool."

The tall lady walked over by the coffee table next to the couch where Turnip lay with his fallen angel. She heaved over and crushed her cigarette in a huge, emerald green ashtray, already full of butts. Then she straightened, wiggled her hips as she adjusted her underwear and hose beneath her elaborate skirt, and cast a leisurely, malevolent stare at Turnip and his teenage lover.

"As for you two, I think you better vamoose. I'm sure that it's been sweet, but me and the mad man here got a few things to toss around."

The tall woman leaned down to cast her eyes at Turnip's face, up-turned now in apprehension toward hers.

"And, little Turnip – I'd suggest that you stop bringing other little vegetables around this particular garden – unless you want yourself weeded out. Am I clear?"

Turnip's face blanched an even whiter shade of pale in the spurious purple light of the room. "Uh, uh, uh, sure, you bet, Miss Moloch, I wasn't thinking, I was partying down there with the locals and little Ida here came up willingly..."

Suddenly the young girl referred to as Miss Ida sprang to life, lifting herself off the couch out of the cross-dresser's lap and flinging back her hair in a most adroit fashion, brown eyes flashing, adjusting her blouse and panties, and directing a cold, sober frown at the strange faces that gaped at her sudden new attitude.

"Alright, that's enough." She swung off the couch, and in a quick movement was on the other side of the room, facing them. As she roughly pulled on her jeans, a radio squawked, and suddenly an automatic pistol was in her hand. A series of yells, screams, and the thuds of logs falling into soft soil sounded outside the cabin. Mad Willie made a move toward a cabinet drawer.

"Hey, fuckhead. Stop, drop, and put up your hands," yelled Little Ida. "All of you – hands behind your heads, and hit the wall!"

The room lit up with high-powered flashlights as Franklin Opano, Tom Mooney, and four uniformed officers smashed into the room.

"FREEZE!" yelled Mooney at the top of his lungs.

"Hey, Tom," said Cowboy, walking in after him. "I think Ida's got it in hand."

"Everybody, hands on the wall – line up!" yelled Ida.

"Yeah, I guess so. Hey, Ida – good job."

"Well, thanks, Tom. I was – hey, wait a minute! Where's Mad Willie?"

Their flashlights swung around. At the back of the large, carpeted and cabinetted room, there was a rock wall – the cabin had been built against the rock outcroppings; they formed the fourth wall. And there, under the high-powered flashlights, an opening could be seen. An opening into a tunnel.

"Shit!" yelled Cowboy. "He's down there, Big Tom."

"Yeah, son. Larson, Kip, and Tonelli, go with him. Guns out, ready to fire. He might have reinforcements, bombs, another lab – who the fuck knows what shit is down in there. As a matter of fact, wait a minute – Officer Grady, get some of those guys from outside and help Ida hook up these jackasses – make sure they're mirandized – read 'em their rights. I'm going down this fucking cave with my kids – outstanding undercover work, Miss Ideen. How long will you look seventeen?"

"Until I'm old enough to retire, Pops. But I did kind of like Turnip. He was almost gentle, especially when he was higher than a kite on that shit he thought I got, after I switched our drinks..."

"Ok, ok, enough kudos. Cowboy, take the lead, son. Yell out a warning as we go in, then – use felony apprehension procedure – consider the perp armed and dangerous, and shoot to kill."

"Understood, Pop. Let's go, fellas."

Cowboy led the group to the rock face, and leaned into the opening cut – a deep defile in the cliff, which was about six feet high and three feet wide, turning immediately downwards, and to the left – where, under the sweep of Cowboy's light, and ancient set of steps appeared, cut into the stone, descending downward and then turning around yet another cut in the rock sixteen feet below, and disappearing.

Cowboy yelled at the top of his lungs: "Attention, attention! Armed officers with search warrant! Lay your weapons on the ground, and come up slowly, with your hands locked behind your head! Respond now, or we will pursue and you will be shot on sight! Respond, now, respond!"

His voice echoed down the stones, and there was no response, only a distant scuffling and the echo of the sound of stones falling.

Cowboy looked back. Behind him stood Tonelli, a young rookie, with an eager grin on his face. "Let's go get 'em, Chief!" whispered Tonelli.

Cowboy looked back past Larson and Kip, both seasoned Nipsak county officers, and made eye contact with his father. Big Tom shrugged. "It's your call, son. But wait one second, before we move."

Mooney keyed his radio. "Opo, how's it going out there? Over."

"Not bad, Manta Ray. We've got the back door shut up here and caught two more driving up in a van with more lab supplies. Ida and her crew just came out the front with the bustheads – what are you guys doing in there? Secure the scene and wait for the evidence tech crew, ok? Over."

"Opo, we've got one on the run – Mad Willie – there's a cavern and a staircase descending into the underground, stair steps and all – me, Tonelli, Kip, and Larson are gonna pursue. We already gave verbal, and have weapons out, over."

"Ok, Tom – lead 'em down. But be advised that's a known felon with assault charges on him – he also did time for attempted. His real name is William John Metopholis Bhoor, and he's got wants and warrants on him from here to Idaho, to Alaska, and… wait one."

The team waited, while Cowboy peered down the passageway, the deputies nervously clicked their hands on their weapons, and Mooney fumed.

"Ok, Tom. I had to intersect calls with DEA and the marshalls' office. You're ok to proceed, under one caveat – take him alive, if at all possible. We've got interstate, and possible international criminal conspiracy grids to work out with this dude. FBI is hovering. Maybe we should just contain suspect and wait him out. We've got a valid field perimeter established. Over."

"Opo, we've got to go down into this cavern. The deputies have flash-bang concussion grenades" – Tom looked at Tonelli, Kip, and Larson, who nodded – "And my son is gonna lead us down there. He's in way better shape than me, and his reflexes are rock solid. Do you approve, over."

"What's Cowboy armed with?"

"An AR-15 laser scope which I'm about to pass up to him, and his county reserve standard sidearm. Over."

"How many years reserve?"

Tom keyed off his mic and whispered up to his son. "Hey, Cowboy."

"Yeah, Pop?"

"How many years you been a reserve?"

"Six, Pop. You oughtta know, you're the one who held me back from regular full time –"

"Yeah, yeah, ok, Hulko. Just relax."

"Fuck you. Let's go get this asshole."

Tonelli, Kip, and Larson grinned. "Yeah, let's go."

Big Tom keyed the mic. "Opo, I'm here on the site and have procedural command. My son is taking point on a pursuit of a fleeing felon, presumably armed. Point possession is the lead assault rifle, an AR-15 equipped with laser scope and metal-jacketed kill rounds. Advise – over."

"Ok, Manta Ray. Chief Bigelow was one of the intersect calls. He agrees, knowing your capabilities regarding designation. Proceed with caution – take alive if possible, and nobody acts like a cowboy. Tell that to the one with the handy nickname. Good luck, and keep the line open. Once again – keep line open. Out."

Big Tom looked to Steve Larson, one of the uniformed deputies, and said, "Unsling your AR, Larson. Fully loaded?"

"Yes, sir. Weapon loaded with kill rounds, extra cartridges on the stock, laser scope charged and ready."

Tom nodded, took the weapon, and moved forward to his son, who was still peering down the precipitous stone stairs.

"What the hell, Dad? Are we going after this fucker? He could be in China by now."

"Yeah, kid, we are. Right now. We had to get approval by the Feds, and the task force. You're gonna lead us down, 'cause I'm too old and too fat, as John Wayne would say. So here's the lead assault weapon, with extra rounds velcroed to the stock – and the laser to the scope. But they want us to take him alive – without undue risk. You familiar with the AR?"

"Yeah, Pop. Range-trained and certified. You were the range officer, remember?"

"Oh, yeah, yeah, ok. Let's give one more warning, then take us down."

"Fuck one more warning. Space 'em out, at five step intervals. I'm low, Larson behind me at mid-range, Kip's high, you're backup. Larson, you got a concussion grenade?"

Deputy Larson handed one up, which Cowboy hooked to a loop on his vest. "Ok, we'll go slow – one flashlight from the back, Kip. I'm gonna switch on the laser. Step carefully, lock and load, and proceed."

"Son, stop," intoned Big Tom. "What is your rank in the reserves?"

"Acting patrol sergeant."

"You are now full sergeant. Alright, proceed."

Cowboy nodded – and lowering his head, followed the beam of his laser scope down the stone steps, one booted foot cautiously following the other, down the sudden turn as the stairway led them into the labyrinth. From far below, there echoed up the sudden sound of maniacal, semi-human laughter – like the soundtrack of an old horror movie.

In front of Big Tom Mooney, Deputy Tonelli farted.

"Oh, shit, not another, Two-horse," muttered Tom.

"Sorry, boss," whispered Tonelli, who promptly farted again. "That's the last of it, I swear."

"For Christ's sake, Tonelli, shut up. We're not the Three Stooges."

Cowboy's forehead was streaming with sweat, even though it was quite cool. He followed the bead of his laser sight down the steps, around the bend, then more steps, then another bend as the stone steps widened to four feet wide, then six feet wide, then – a distant, glowing, diffuse yellow light. He held up his hand, and the team halted. The stairway was now as wide as a man was tall, and the ceiling of the passageway also was growing in height. Ahead was another turn, towards the weirdly diffuse yellow light. Cowboy turned off the laser scope, and flattened his back against the cavern wall, opposite the light source. His team followed suit. He looked back, motioned them to stay put, poked two fingers at his eyes to indicate he was going to take a look at what was around the expanded bend in the rock, and slid forward.

"HAH, HA, HAH, HAH, HA HA HA!"

Sudden insane laughter filled the stairway, blowing up from the large cavern below and spooking the hell out of every horse in the war party. Deputy Tonelli almost pissed his pants; Deputy Kip let off an involuntary blast of cuss words; Deputy Larson hit himself in the head with the barrel of his shotgun; Cowboy fell flat to the ground, and Big Tom almost dropped a load in his drawers.

"HAH! HAH! HA, HA, HA, HA, HA, HA, HAH! SEND IN A BATTLE SCAR, SEND IN THE TANKS!" roared the crazy voice. "Have the buffalo herd checked for fleas, dog trots, and fettuccini, have the troops inspected for coozle worms and syphilis! Give 'em each a rifle, cut off an arm, and send 'em down the sewer line to terrorize the town! HAR, HAR, HAR!"

Cowboy clicked on his laser, pulled out his concussion grenade, and, propped up on his elbows, looked back at his patrol. Everybody was wide-eyed, blanch-faced, and freaked out – unknowing. Everybody except Big Tom, who was slowly moving forward, down the steps along the cave wall, approaching Cowboy's position with a knowing look on his face. He crouched next to his son, and whispered, "I know this guy. I'd know that voice anywhere. That's crazy Ollie."

"YAR, HAR HAR! EARLY GRIMES LOOKED AT THE TIMES WHICH WAS A BIG DIRTY WASTE AND THEN HE PUNCHED HIMSELF IN THE FIST WITH HIS FACE! HAR, HAR, YAR, YAR, YAR!"

Cowboy looked up at his dad. "What the fuck? Who is he? Is he the guy we're after, Pop?"

"Well, no, fuck no, I just can't believe that, Junior. This guy, if it is who I think it is, is your second cousin."

"What?!?"

"OH, WILLARD WAS A CARPENTER, HE HAMMERED NAILS AND PLANKS" howled the voice – "AND WHEN HE WAS A'FINISHED, NEVER GOT A WORD OF THANKS! SO EARLY GRIMED WENT DOWN WITH THE TIMES, AND STEPPED INTO HIS GRAVE, AND LOOKED INTO THE UNDERTAKER'S EYE AND STOLE BACK ALL THE MONEY HE'D NEVER SAVED. HAR, HAR, YAR, HAR, HAR!"

The voice of the mad man suddenly seemed closer to their position.

Larson hollered, "What do we do, Chief?" He dropped protocol and brought his weapon to bear on the enlarged entry that curved into the dimly lit cavern.

Cowboy tensed, and sent his laser light into fire search pattern. Big Tom put his hand between his son's shoulder blades, said "Wait," and stood up on the last stone step which led into the eerie light.

"Crazy Ollie!" he hollered. "Ollie George Lightfoot, is that you? It is I, Manta-Ray from the old boat landing. You remember, Ollo – down on the summertime rock beach between Jeff's Head and the old landing piers! Is that you, Oliver Snakeskin?"

There ensued a large pause from below, then a sound like the shortage of a dragon clearing his nostrils after blowing some fire out of his nose."

"MANTA-RAY? IS that the voice of an ancient turncoat traitor I hear? If so, step forward, insane hallucination, and I will destroy you – yea, verily I will blast you out of your shoes, ghost! Who dares invade my inner sanctum with voices from the past? BEGONE, I TELL YOU – BEGONE, THE LOT OF YA! I'LL BRING FORTH THE WRATH OF YATES, AND BETWEEN HE AND SPRECKLES, YOU WILL BE DESTROYED!"

"Shit, Pop," spouted Cowboy. "That crazy fuck just mentioned Spreckles! Damn! Do you think that – "

"Hold on, son."

Tom looked back at the waiting deputies, who were now thoroughly spooked.

"Just hold on, guys. Hang tight and hold fire. I know this guy – I'm going in."

Cowboy started to struggle up from his prone firing position, and Big Tom touched his son again on his shoulder.

"Just hold your position, Sergeant. Back me up on signal, but hold fire – this ain't our perp."

And before Cowboy could stop him, Big Tom Mooney walked around the last stone step and down into the cavern.

"Hello, Crazy Ollie. What's shaking, old buddy? Are the fish biting?"

As his father's back disappeared around the shadowy rocks, Cowboy rose up and cautiously signaled his men forward, following his father's lead.

They stepped into a huge cavern with an uneven floor of tumbled boulders, some as big as houses. A strange array of fat-belled candles and old railroad lanterns lit their way. In the middle of the place stood a very large, hooded, cloaked figure, dressed in greasy rags, with a messy dark beard flowing out of his face. His eyebrows jumped in astonishment as he flailed his arms and danced backwards away from Tom Mooney, who advanced upon him in a slow, confident pace. The hooded giant then stopped, crossed his arms, and stamped his foot.

"IF YOU ARE TOM MOONEY, WHO I KNEW AS MAN-TA-RAY WHEN I WAS A CHILD, SAY OUT NOW THE THREE PRAYERS THAT WE USED TO SING IN THE WOODS BEFORE WE VENTURED INTO THE DARK WATERS OF THE SOUND!"

Without hesitation, Tom replied, in a calm, loud voice: "Hey, big trees, watch over me. Hey, stupid crows, tell us what you know. Hey, scary tide, tell us where to hide."

Then Tom faced the apparition, folded his arms over his chest in a likewise manner, coughed, looked down between his feet, and spit. "And that is all we need to fill the bill and do the deed."

"HA! HA, HA, HA, HAR, HAR, HAR, YAR YAR YAR!" roared the giant and she threw back his hood and rushed forward to embrace Mooney.

"By God, Manta-Ray, it really is you! Where have you been, my brother? And who are these miniature people in uniforms, carrying fake fishing poles. You know, I can kill them with a flick of my wrist."

"STOP!" yelled Tom as Cowboy's laser-spot danced across the chest of the crazy robed stranger. "I grew up with this man, this is Oliver Wendall George. Ollie, this is my son, who we call Cowboy, and his friends, Deputies Tonelli, Kip, and Larsen. Guns down, boys. This is a friend, and tribal cousin. We will sit with him, and talk, and see what we will see. Larsen, and Kip — secure the area, weapons ready. Tonelli — go toward that hole on the other side of the cavern and hold it. Son, approach — and let us talk with an old tribal warrior."

Oliver Wendall George sat down on a large, flat rock, and eye Big Tom Mooney ominously. "Why have you brought these miniature people here, my old friend? I came here to be crazy on my own, eat the fish in the spring rivers, and surface only in the summers when the other fools follow the snowmelt from the glaciers above — here I sought peace, and to eventually die alone, as a warrior."

"Oliver..."

"Please, Manta-Ray. Call me by my old name. It has been so long."

"Ok, Chiquota, before we came down into your view, did you see a man, a crazy-looking man with a big head shaped like a pumpkin?"

"You mean Mad Willie?"

"You know him?"

"Yes, yes, those assholes have a meth lab up above. They tried to come down here before, a couple of times last year – I caught one, strangled him to within an inch of his life, and sent him back up to warn the others not to descend into my realm again – but they did, of course. So I made a deal."

"What kind of deal, Crazy Ollie?"

"Well, I told them not to pollute my cavern with their filthy shit or I would kill them to within an inch of their life, then torture the rest. But they didn't listen. One night they came down the ancient stairway, and tried to burn me out as I slept. But I was ready for them. I caught one and bent his head, and was going to twist another one into a pretzel, but then Spreckles came and stopped me. He made them go away, back up the stairs, and told me that better days were coming."

Crazy Ollie stopped talking, drew his greasy hood up over his shaggy haed, and regarded Big Tom with his gigantic eyes. "Do you remember Spreckles, Manta-Ray?"

Mooney coughed, shifted his gun to his left hand, and took out a pack of cigarettes. "Sure I do, Crazy Ollie. You want a smoke?"

"I quit, Manta-Ray. Many years ago. And so should you."

The large, yellow-brown, bear-like eyes flickered. Tom put the cigarettes away without lighting one.

"So you are saying that Al-Indeska-Chiuk was here? In this cavern? And he stopped you from killing Pumpkinhead Mad Willie and his meth-lab friends? Who were trying to invade your space?"

"Exactly, Manta-Ray. That is why, when he ran through here earlier, just before you came down, I sent Pumpkin on his way and waited for the rest of those nincompoops to come bopping into my cave – you should have just let me do my thing and you would have never had to bother with them again."

"Wait a minute, Oliver. When the guy you call Pumpkinhead, also known as Mad Willie, also know as…"

"Yeah, yeah, yeah, Manta-Ray. Also known as asshole of the world. He came through here just before you, spouting his shit. Tried to set me up to take you guys out, move some big rocks around, make you take a fall. But I wasn't buying it, so I sent him on his way."

"Wait, Ollie, you sent him…"

"Yeah, man. I moved some rocks around. He's right over there, underneath that rock that your yellow-haired deputy is standing on – what's his name, Law-son? He looks nervous with that shotgun. Maybe you should take it away from him, give him a smaller gun. Maybe, like a water pistol –"

"Larson!" barked Big Tom.

"Yeah?"

"Check under that rock you're standing on – look for human remains."

"What? Uh, what, man?"

"Recent human remains, Larson. And make sure it's dead."

"Oh, it's dead, Manta-Ray. I moved some rocks, put his ass under," said Crazy Ollie. "His ass is gone. Won't bother us no more. But you can tell your miniature friend there, Deputy Lawson dog, to quit trying to move rocks that he can't move. Pumpkinhead ain't down there. Pumpkinhead is in a deeper place – and you'd need ten bulldozers and fifty miniature men to even start to find him. And another thing, Manta-Ray – about Spreckles."

Big Tom shifted his bulk on the rock he was sitting on and perked up his ears. He was cognizant of his son, Cowboy, who had silently moved up and now stood beside him, with the AR-15 held at port arms.

"Hey! Ol' Manta-Ray! Your son is not so miniature, hey? He looks good – like a warrior from the days before we sold out to the casinos! Ok, so I will tell you – Al-Indeska-Chiuk – who we knew as Spreckles – is sailing now under the stars. You won't catch him with miniatures, and you doubt him at your own false reasons – he knows more than you. One step ahead, or behind you. What you say in your radios is already in his hearing – he knows the Salish Sea, and all the tribes. He has visited more than you by water. Also – lately he has been going about dressed as a woman in a green gown – calling himself Molach, or Miss Molach. Something like that. However, now that Big Pumpkin is gone, and Little Turnip is busted – I predict Al-Indeska will end his cross dressing ways and return to other disguises – as I myself will now fling off these greasy, caveman clothes and ascend out of this fucking ditch that I've been living in. Would you guys like to lead the way up out of here? And, Deputy Larson – tell Tonelli and Kip they can stop looking at me like I'm a nut case. Just because I'm 6'8" tall and weigh 190 pounds, doesn't mean I'm not a tribal cop – does it, Manta-Ray? By the way, Chief Bigelow sends his regards and told me to tell you that it was him that won that wrestling match on the beach – not you.

"Can we go? I'm hungry. Let's hit the nearest McDonalds when we get the fuck up out of here. What do you say? What is it, forty miles to Belfair?"

The back wall of the cavern held a flickering light as a sudden shadow crossed, then vanished. There was a low rumble of falling rock.

"And there goes Al-Indeska-Chiuk, or Spreckles, if you want – or the one the vegetables know as Miss Molach. We won't be seeing him again for a while."

Cowboy and Big Tom both started to move, but Crazy Ollie reached out a bear paw and stopped them. "Forget it, fellas. I taught him how to move rocks. The way is shut, now, to that particular passage. And even if it weren't, I wouldn't let you chase him. Resistance is futile. Don't worry too much about it – all will be revealed. Now, shall we go up? I'm hungry as a fucking bear – I want some MEAT! I'm a little tired of eating fish every fucking day."

And so they climbed out of there, up the ancient stairway, Oliver Wendall George bringing up the rear, snuffing out candles and collecting lanterns as he came.

Of course, he left a few. For the next intrepid visitors.

Chapter 14

Nancy woke up as the plane was beginning its landing approach and was momentarily confused. What city was this that they were flying in to? She struggled out of sleep and realized her hair was caught in the leather jacket of the man sitting next to her, who was snoring. He was sporting a three-day beard and dragon breath, along with cascading blond hair and a tiny tattoo of a sword clutched in a fist on the side of his neck.

Oh, shit, she thought. I've been sleeping with Roots Calvino, our replacement bass player. Oh shit, oh shit, oh shit. I mean – it's okay to fall asleep together on a long plane flight after a thirty-five-city tour, but to actually have slept with the son-of-a-bitch last night in the hotel room…

It all came back to her, as the plane cruised slowly around the airport, altitude descending along with the celebratory high of their last gig. My God, she thought. I'm a mother. I'm a wife. I have love back home, where I'm returning to now. I have responsibilities other than making a name for myself in the big lights, the bright stages, the yells and scream of approval of thousands of people who don't even know me. Oh shit, oh my God. I'm a piglet, and I want my pig. I want to hold my girl-child. Oh crap, oh Jesus, oh what have I done. I've got money in my pocket, my name in the newspapers, and my soul is in the sewer. Oh, Cowboy, oh, Chiquiti, please forgive me. Little girl, my Hoquiam, please don't let me go. I swear I'll make it up to you, oh please God don't let me lose my family…

The airplane continued to circle in long, mind-numbing curves over the Seattle airport known as Sea-Tac. And Nancy continued to suffer her reticent reaction. She was getting more anxious, and more awake, by the minute. Her slumbering seatmate slumbered on, snoring, breathing his whisky fumes into the side of her face. She turned away in disgust, pulling her hair out of the tangle of his coat, and stared out the window at the myriad lights of Seattle, and the darkness of the forests beyond, toward the Nipsak Peninsula, the foothills of the Olympic Mountains, her home. Or – what she hoped was still her house.

Oh my God, oh, god, oh my only one, her thoughts pounded in the suddenly lit caverns of her heart. What have I done? I haven't been home in 60 days! I haven't kissed my daughter, held her, laughed with her in the sunshine, and looked into the dark brown eyes of my Cowboy, in 60 – no, almost 90 days!

As soon as he looks in my eyes, forest brown looking into forest green, he'll know that I've been unfaithful – ah, shit, it sounds so corny. Then why is my heart falling to the floor of my stomach in dread?

The memory of the last day and night whirled through her mind – a triumphant last show, showering applause, the intensity of the chorus of their encore song:
"I want
one for the heartache
two for the kiss
three for the thousands
of lies you told me and
four for the miss.
I want
five for the damages
that you know you've done.
I want
six bullets of freedom
loaded in my freedom gun."
But now in her heart she sang, mournfully –
"Hey, star-child
Somewhere among the planets
You're running wild.
Hey, can you
Trust the seed
That makes you
See the need
In me.

Hey, wandering soul
Can you stop running
On those back roads.
Kiss me before
I'm too old
And I'll give you
My soul to hold."

A little bell dinged, and the pilot's voice, deep and soothing, came over the P.A. "Well, folks, we're making our final approach into Sea-Tac Airport. Please make sure you are seated with your seatbelts firmly fastened. At this time all flight attendants should be likewise seated. The temperature in Seattle is 42°, windy and rainy – to those of you who live here, welcome home – to those you continuing on south with us, please stay seated as there is no layover. Thank you for flying with us, and have a wonderful…"

Nancy turned to look at Captain Beefhead, Ronnie "Roots" Calvino. He had some drool trickling into his beard. *My God, what was I thinking?*

As they deplaned and were walking up the concourse, her road manager and agent both were making noises about rehearsals, an upcoming television appearance, requests from the band for more money, label contracts – but all she could hear in her head was the second chorus to the song:

"I want
one for the busted home
two for the kids
three for the millions of lies you told
and four for the miss.
I want
Five for the renegade
That you've become.
I want
Six bullets of freedom
Loaded in my freedom gun."

The rain streaking the windows of the terminal looked like endless running tears, and as she walked out in the rush of the cold, wet wind and the noise of the tires splashing, she suddenly knew that she had to tell Cowboy everything. Make it or break it, she thought – I'm not going to live a lie. Besides, he'll be able to tell, anyway. He can read me like a living book.

Her band mates rallied around her in a happy, tired, and relieved mushiness, kissing, hugging, questioning – "Are you OK, babe?"

"Yeah, just tired," then a sudden bear-hug from behind, and a leathery, bearded stench – Ronnie "Roots" Calvino. "It was great, honey. But don't worry – I won't tell no one," he whispered in her ear.

"Fuckin-A you won't, slime ball, or I'll kill you," she said out loud, squirming out of his arms. "Don't worry, everybody. We'll use Ronnie's parts in the studio that are already on tape, if he ends up dead. Right, Roots?"

"Uh, yeah, sure. Hey man, you know, shit…"

Nancy relented at the sight of his big, dumb, confused eyes, so worrisome. "Oh, don't fret, you big baby. We've all got a week off!" Nancy faced her band, seven beautiful musicians, all tried and true. Then she kissed them, one by one (except Roots), and told them she'd organize a studio session in a week or so, to start working on the next CD. "Great tour, everybody! Now, let's go home!"

There was a ragged cheer and they all scattered to the equipment carts to pick up their instruments and personal gear.

As Nancy watched them go, Charlie/Charlene walked up and stood next to her. "Pretty good group," she huffed, in a husky, high tenor voice. "Not the best we've had – I miss that crazy Australian."

"Yeah, well, ya know. Letting an equipment van roll over your foot will put you in a cast every time. Hey, listen. What's everybody saying about me spending the night with Calvino?"

"Not a hell of a lot. They all like him; he's not a snake. He shows up on time even when he's hungover and doesn't miss a note. He's just young, dumb, and full of… Oh, shit. Sorry. Look – it just happened, you know? Hot tub fury. Motel meltdown. It wasn't close to rape, I can tell you that – You were smoking Fell-Mells like the rest of us and threw your panties into the breeze before I did."

Nancy grimaced. "What the fuck are Fell-Mells?"

"Roll-your-own cigarettes with a strong muscle relaxer and killer pot. You were mixing it with champagne cocktails."

"Shit, Charlene. I balled that big idiot and didn't even remember it until I woke up on the plane."

"Girl, we carried you onto the plane. Just about. Airport security wanted to put you into observation. I had to pass out a lot of free CDs and promising tickets to your next tour dates."

"Was I acting crazy?"

"No, out comatose. Heavy-lidded eyes, slurred speech, all that. TSA let us pass you through the VIP lounge incognito. Although, some young executive-banker type dude who had a lot of pull recognized you, and helped grease the wheels. You gave him a big, sloppy kiss."

"SHIT, Charlene! That's not me! That is NOT me! I'm a wife, I'm a mom, I'm a..."

"Darlin', you're an exhausted pop star coming home from a grueling tour. Now, get in that limo, and we'll take you to the shuttle – Cowboy called and is not picking you up."

"Wait – what?" Nancy quickly checked her Blackberry. "He didn't call me..."

"Nope, bad girl, and I'll tell you why. He texted me with an urgent message – him and his dad got some kind of big cop thing going – way the hell out there in the boonies, beyond where you live. He didn't want to leave a dedicated message on your line – don't ask me why, 'cause I don't know. Now, c'mon, Nancy. I'm just as tired as you. And I did some crazy fucking things in that hotel last night too, ya know."

"Charlene, did me and you? Ya know..."

"Nope. You wanted pig meat, so you flopped with old Ronnie. I wanted delectables, so I went to the room of the keyboard girl – we keyed her, and she wasn't bored. So to speak."

Nancy looked wan, and confused, then got it and laughed out loud like a horse.

"Dammit, Charl! You can always cut away the anvils, make me feel better.."

"I know, Nance. Now, let's get in the limo. It's cold, we are wet, and you've got a shuttle to catch. On the way, we'll talk about Hoquiam and Cowboy."

"Hoquiam! You said Cowboy's on a cop thing, a dispatch! Where's Hoqi?"

"At your sister's. Your mom's there, too. It's all in the text message – here, read it while I put your guitar in the trunk."

The limo had been waiting in the VIP pickup area so long, an airport cop had his ticket book out. Charlene schmoozed him, and they avoided the ticket, settling back in the luxurious leather. As they cruised into the roundabout traffic, Nancy read Cowboy's message:

Piglet – Me and Pop get to go into the woods tonight and flank some donuts, arrest some vegetables – Hoquiam with sis and mom – see you tomorrow, but – don't go home! Stay with sis until I call – Pig. P.S. – T.M. may call before I do. P.S.S. – You I love.

Nancy squinted at the last words, coughed, and burst into tears. The rain streaked down the windshields. She joined it, and sang sad music while Charlie squeezed her hand.

The shuttle van was waiting on the outskirts of the airport – it left every hour, 24-7, taking the few late-night passengers who were heading to the far reaches of Nipsak County on the two-hour ride. For only sixteen dollars, however, the vans had comfortable seats, soft music, low lights to sleep by or spots to read by, and good coffee and tea. Kind of like a tiny, wheeled airplane, driving over the Tacoma Narrows bridge, past Gig Harbor and on into the sparsely populated areas. In two hours, Nancy would be at a tiny four-corners called Nipsak Fold, where at least one local taxi could be called (in advance, by the van driver) and take her up into the hills to her home.

She said goodbye to Charlie, who gave her a hug, kiss, and encouraging smile, and settled back for a long ride of remorse and indecision about what to say – how to say – when to say – should I say – what will he say – please, oh, please, don't get pissed off and go away – it's not a heartbreaker! I don't want it to be! What if his price is to go out and fuck around with some local cop groupies? Nah – he's never been like that.

But he's never had me screw around on him – shit! Maybe I won't tell him. What if he wants a separation? What if this gets in the music news stream, the papers? What if... Oh, Hoquiam, I need to hold you... I'm still Mom... I'm still Piglet... I'm still... I'm still... I'm still...

She fell asleep, and the van drove through the wind and the rain.

Chapter 15

The screen door slammed behind Ashina as she bent down on the darkened, old wood porch to get more firewood. Hoquiam stood just inside, watching the trees and leaves fly around in the wind and the rain. Suddenly, there was Bones the dog, quietly nuzzling her from the side. She dropped to her knees and hugged him, carefully moving aside into the darkness as Ashina, grunting with the effort of carrying an armload of firewood. The new wood tumbled onto the fireplace hearth as Hoqi went forward and tugged at Ashini's skirt.

"Huh? Oh, it's you, is it, you little squatch. Back to bed you go. Geneva! Hoqi's up, musta snuck out of bed. You, dog – out on the porch."

"Noooo," said Hoquiam, hugging the dog. He looked up at Ashina, hopefully wagging his tail.

"All right, flea-bag – under there, then," she pointed an adamant finger under the couch. The dog dropped his butt on the floor, flopped out his tongue, and grinned, still secure in Hoqi's embrace.

"Not there, Nana! In bed with me! Mama said…"

Just then her aunt Geneva swept in and took Hoqi up in her arms. She had long dark hair and a slim figure, smaller than her sister's, with dark brown eyes instead of Nancy's green.

"OK, Hoqums. Quit trying to hustle your Gran-ma. Bones, under the couch. Now!"

Old Bones, defeated by Aunt Geneva's righteous propriety, crept under the couch with a groan and a regretful look at Hoquiam, who burst into tears.

"Noooo! He can't fit under there, Auntie Gen!"

Sure enough, the couch began to heave upwards under the old dog's efforts to obey the fearful, tribal women's orders. Damn Wimmen! He thought. I wanna be with Hoqi! Why they wanna keep us apart? I can't fit under this couch, but I'll try. I better get my food on time tomorrow, dammit. Doggone it. And it better not be that shitty Indian lard and scrap shit – I like the new, modern food that Ol' Cowboy gives me. Canned. Hoqi likes it, too. Sometimes, when nobody's lookin', she gets down and eats it with me out of the bowl…

Thus thought the dog, Bones, believe it or not. But – why not believe it? Wouldn't a dog have thoughts just as these?

After Hoquiam, wailing and pointing at the dog in tragic loss over Geneva's shoulder, was carried off to bed, Ashina picked up the couch, said, "Uh-unett-ak-eh" in a guttural voice, and Bones skedaddled out the screen door, which he opened with his baseball-sized nose, and curled up next to the woodpile. "Well, good dog," she said, a little surprised. Relenting, she went to the fridge, took out a soup-bone, and tossed it out on the porch.

After a second, there was a shuffling, then a contented gnawing, crunching sound commenced, which she knew would last for hours, as he tried to get to the marrow. The screen door slammed one last time, and then the solid old six-panel door slammed shut on the stormy, early spring night. A modicum of domestic quiet fell inside the reservation house, as the flames snapped in the stone fireplace and the un-insulated oak boards of the floor creaked underfoot. No trailer, this – no mobile home up on blocks – this was one of the old places that were built by hand back in the old days. It had been in the Chiquiti family since the beginning. Or – the so-called beginning. The old, old new beginning. Before anyone even knew the word "casino" and gambling was done with cards, boards, sticks, and wampum. Sometimes hides, special food, or certain weapons or clothes. But gently, and never for blood, or money, or the rights to steal land from someone. All right – maybe not always "gently" – and maybe sometimes drunkenly. All right – maybe, on rare occasions, fights arose, even a killing or two. But – nobody had ever heard of the word "casino".

Geneva came back into the living room as Anisha was replacing the couch and settling herself into it, under an old, purple woolen blanket.

"She went asleep, asking for Bones, Nancy, and Cowboy, in that order."

"Uh-huh. She loves that dog more than them, I think. And no wonder – Cowboy's out with old Big Tom, trying to be a hero. And as for
Nancy, Miss Big-Time-Too-Proud-To-Call Music Star…"

"Mama! She called you last week! You told me!"

"Yeah, on that cell-phone thing. I hate those fucking things. Why
can't she call me on the Earth-line?"

"It's land-line, Mom. And she's busy out there. I think it's great. I'm
not jealous."

"Oh, no? Not jealous? I heard that you were bitching to Chinada
just the other day about the fact that your sister was gonna make more
money this year than you'll make in your lifetime…"

"Well, yeah, I was, and it's probably true. But I'm happy with Mac
Stallworth, he pays pretty good. I just got a raise, and I've only been
there two years."

"Humph. Doing the books for a plumbing company when you're as
talented as your sister. I blame it all on Spreckles. If you hadn't stood
up for that fool when nobody else would, your name wouldn't have a
mark against it on the tribal register…"

"That's enough, Mom." Geneva adjusted the volume on the baby
monitor she held in her hand, bringing the soft, gurgling sounds of
Hoquiam's breathing into the room.

"And let's not call him Spreckles. Al-Indeska Chuik is more than my
half-brother – he is descended from the true blood line of Chief Sealth
and the longboat rowers, who unified the tribes of the Salish Sea. Why
do you hate him so?"

"Because he killed your grandmother, my mother-in-law, who just
didn't see it coming."

"That's bullshit, and you know it. I happen to know that Franklin,
Cowboy, and Big Tom are working with him, undercover, to flush out
a big drug gang up in the lost swamp of DeWatto, as we speak."

"Are you insane, Geneva? Have your feet grown too big for your moc-
casins? Are you a white Indian? Listen to me, Al-Ishka-She. Spreckles
is no good; he causes trouble wherever he goes. Just the fact that the
tribe has found out that he's still alive after all these years we thought
him dead and gone, and good riddance…"

"Mother, you're a stupid old hen. Chiukis is going to clear his name, and go down in the tribal register as a hero, and a standup warrior. If you don't believe me, ask Cowboy and Big Tom, tomorrow. Tonight they are out there, tearing it up with my other half-brother, Opo Franklin, and Chief Bigelow and the rest to get to the bottom of the source of these sickening drugs that have been coming in to all the rez's lately. Everybody's talking about it."

"Yeah, everybody's talking. Nobody knows shit. If you ask me, the casinos were the best thing that ever happened. All across the country, tribes are building huge, beautiful casinos. Why, just last month they finished pouring the concrete for the one up in Snoqualmie. My cousin Judy Chiquiti is involved with trying to build another in Tulalip…"

"You are sorely misguided, Mother. Those gigantic casinos will not enrich all of their tribal members – just some. The one in Snoqualmie is going to give up 60 acres of land to buildings, and another 60 acres to parking lots and facilities – with most of the jobs in construction going to outsiders, and tribal elders and family royals giving up future land rights to leverage optional development deals – and tribe member populations gets a lot less than they should. They throw some new pickup trucks at them, a couple of shitty new houses. What about the future? What about ongoing medical, dental clinics, new schools? Do you see those things happening? No, it's all big casinos – white people coming to gamble away their pensions, drunks in wheelchairs getting escorted out who then file lawsuits, and of course – tribal police making a killing on busting the fools who drive out of the parking lots on their lips at three in the morning, trying to make it the two miles back to their hotel rooms."

"What – you think they make money on that?"

"I don't know."

"Well, Clearwater just added on a new hotel. So that will take care of the drunk drivers."

"Mom, are you crazy? They do it anyway! People who get drunk and lose money in casinos want to drive out onto the roads just to prove they haven't lost everything, that they still have some control over their actions."

"Right. And that's when our tribal police nab 'em, and turn 'em over to the county for processing. The county sheriffs put 'em in the pokey, and those fools pay a hefty fine."

"Yes, Mom. That's what casinos are for. Robbing fools not once, not twice, but three times. And the tribes get what?"

"You're a foolish girl, Geneva."

"Mom, do you know that one of my best friends is a tribal shift supervisor at Kon-A-Paw Hotel Casino, and she has a gambling problem so bad that she's in the hole and owes management at least 60% of her next four paychecks, and they still encourage her to gamble? Did you know that?"

"That's enough, Kal-An-Chi. That's enough. I know the casinos have changed everything around here, but I also know that you weren't around when the shit hit the fan before you were born. I love you, but that's enough for tonight. Now, let's go to bed."

Geneva looked at her mother's stern, careworn, wrinkled face. There was a tiny smile at the corner of her lips.

"OK, Mom," she sighed. "OK, Anisha. Let's agree on that."

They went to their bedrooms, the lights in the house went out, the flames died down in the old stone fireplace, and outside on the old wooden porch, the gnawing sounds continued as the dog Bones searched for the marrow, as his kind have done since the beginning of dog time.

Chapter 16

"All right, my name is Franklin Opano, Naval Criminal Investigation Division, and I'm going to call this meeting to order. Please, everybody take a seat. Thank you. To my left, you see Thomas Mooney, Nipsak County Special Investigator. To my right, George Bigelow, senior tribal elder and one of the leading chiefs of the Salish Indian Nations – next to him, Sergeant William Tonelli of the Nipsak County Drug Enforcement, whose son was recently part of a raid team which netted quite a few vegetables and shut down a major drug manufacturing laboratory. Next to him, Cowboy Mooney, Tom's son, leader of that team and recently brought into full time law enforcement from the Nipsak County Sherrif's Department Reserve, now with the rank of full sergeant and special investigator. Next to him, Harry Box, Metropolitan Crime Squad, working witht eh guy next to him, our liaison from Canada, Special Lieutenant Samuel Crowdell, and going up the other side of the table, we have Drug Enforcement Agent Sintell Lewis; next to her, Nipsak County Sheriff's Drug Enforcement Division liaison Sherry Passarelli; and next to her, Jim Nighthawk, representing the tribal casinos.

"Now, everybody comfortable? Got your coffee, your tea, your water, your antacid tablets, whatever? Good. 'Cause I'm gonna launch into a little speech here, and then we're going to watch a film. Visual aids, we used to call it. But it ain't pretty, ladies and gentlemen. No, it ain't pretty, by anybody's imagination.

"We all know why we are here – it's about drugs. Now, there are many enforcement teams specializing in the eradication of methamphetamine manufacturing laboratories here, and I know we've worked extensively with some of you here.

"No, the problem here is not methamphetamine. And the reason the United States Navy is involved is three-fold. First, because this new drug which we are going to learn about seems to be specifically targeted at US Navy personnel – specifically, in the counties of Nipsak and Mason; Nipsak, where many enlisted active duty sailors live in rented housing while their ships are in port, and Mason, where many of them go to party – 'out in the boonies', away from the possibly scrutiny of family, fellow sailors who are not so inclined, and, because of its extreme rural, spread-out nature, they are less apt to be observed in criminal drug activity.

"But then, after a few days of these 'beachside location-rations', as they call them, these sailors, usually low-ranking – we've seen none above the rank of first class petty officer, and most emerging spec-2 – they return to their rented homes, which they share with shipmates, wives, or, rarely, civilian friends and go on a rampage. And when I say rampage, I mean it – literal mayhem, involving assault with great bodily injury, self-mutilation, assault in public. Was at a recent 7-11 store attempted murder with an ax, with attempt to kill, and domestic violence toward family members – mainly wives and children, but parents, and grandparents also, who happen to live in the area – which have resulted in the deaths of two civilians and three naval personnel in the last 26 months. The Navy has seen fit to appoint myself as the lead special investigative officer on the task force, which we have seated here today, to look into the matter.

By the way, my naval rank is Lieutenant Commander, but you can just call me Opo. Just don't open a can o' worms when you call me for dinner..."

Laughs around the table. Opo leaned forward with a new intensity, an involvement to draw them in. They responded, leaning forward, eyes wide open, drawing in his information, brows furrowed, notepads and Palm Pilots forgotten.

"Now, listen. Meth is nothing compared to this new drug that is being manufactured. Crack cocaine is like popcorn compared to this shit. As best as our scientists can ascertain, from autopsies and blood samples from the few users who stay alive long enough to be able to give blood samples, this stuff takes the human brain and nervous system to a place it's never been before. Forget LSD, forget the best marijuana you ever smoked." A few nervous laughs. "Forget cocaine, the best you ever snorted." Dead silence. "And forget heroin, or morphine, or any kind of crazy, half-poison meth shit that the biker gang labs cook up.

"They call this stuff 'frac'. Short for 'fracture'. It is cooked up with chemical compounds which elicit extreme, immediate pleasure that is on an intensity level that is 100 times to one over the purest cocaine, and meth isn't even in the ballpark. One snort, one inhaled smoke or ingested powder hit of this product and the chemistry of the brain is immediately changed forever. And I don't mean that in a good way. Now, we are about to watch a series of film clips which have been compiled in the last few months showing various local city, county, and state police departments across the country where security cameras in such places as grocery store, malls, sporting goods stores, schools, gas stations, and places like Home Depot have taken 911 reports and responded to violent criminal behavior. As I mentioned earlier – it is extreme, to be specific – you will se a man suddenly grab a large wood ax off an equipment display shelf in a Home Depot and chase a woman down the aisle, finally catching her, hacking at her neck and head, and then turning on other customers who come to help her, grievously injuring two of them, before police officers knock him out from both sides with tasers and night sticks. The only reason he wasn't shot is because the first responding team of local police officers were tackled by his friend, who was shot, but only after he cut off one of the cops' hands. That's right – the perp wacked off the cop's hand.

"Now, in a similar incident, in a mall, a man and his young son were chased after three men asked to test out their latest picks and shovels. One of the men also tried to start a demonstrator model chainsaw, which of course did not contain fuel. So he used it as a battering ram. In this incident, the father of the child put himself over the boy, sustaining major back injuries ; the metal blades ripped right through to his lungs as well, almost killing him. He survived, will be disable the rest of his life, and of course the boy is permanent traumatized.

"Well, I could go on with this horrific narrative, however, suffice be it to say – all of these violent assaults which I have described have been perpetrated by low to mid-ranking naval personnel on temporary leave while their ships were berthed at nearby naval bases, and all of the said perpetrators in subsequent interviews after their apprehension had absolutely no memory of their actions and were horrified to learn that they were responsible for this mayhem. In fact, in spite of suicide watches while incarcerated and awaiting arraignment, one of these sailors managed to commit suicide.

"All right, there is your preliminary overview of the situation, ladies and gentlemen. At the conclusion of this film compilation, we will be joined by secure video uplink by representatives of Homeland Security, the Federal Bureau of Investigation, the regional superior officers commanding in the US Navy, and a liaison from the DEA.

"Yes, my friends. This is a very big deal. This is vector priority. These termites must be stopped. Now, lights out, please. Let us begin the film."

Chapter 17

The boat was tossed as it went crosswise to an incoming tidal current wave. The sun had disappeared behind Mt. Skokomish, and Chiuk Indeska, also known as Spreckles and Miss "Morock" Moloch, among other names, guided it into a tiny inlet with an inborn skill. He plopped over the side in his rubber boots, and shoved the fourteen-foot sloop up onto the rocky beach, as darkness descended. The only lights showing were distant, scattered houses miles away down the Hood Canal beach. He was alone. Above him, a forest canopy of maple and alder, lifting into forests of fir and cedar – behind him, the small and gentle waves breaking on the beach, which could become quite large, and dangerous, in the storms which frequently battered the region.

Chiuk pulled out a cell phone and speed-dialed a number.

"Nooksak," said a voice. "What took you so long to call? I've been waiting."

"Well, wait a little longer, Ping-Pong. They hit Pumpkin and Turnip, and got all the vegetables weeded out. Now, your boys are competition free. But, you better relocate your lab. I think that one of them rot-heads might know where you're at – and you know they're all gonna cop-puke out everything they know to try to plea-bargain. Hey – did you know that Turnip was a girl?"

"No, man, he's not a girl. He just likes to cross-dress when he gets high."

"Actually, no, Pong-Bong. The task force cops strip-searched him before they put him in the wagon – and he did have a dildo strapped on under his dress – but, when they got right down under the panties – there was nothing there but a pussy. With two ounces of frac in plastic bags stuffed up it."

"Wow – I would've liked to have been the cop who pulled those out of there. I betcha they smelled sweet."

Chiuk held the phone away from his face, and frowned at it, his eyes almost crossing involuntarily.

"Yeah, right, Ping. That is how sick you are. I keep forgetting."

"Where are you? I need hourly updates…"

"Hey, fuck you, homes. The only thing you are gonna get from me is what I said originally – inside information. If you want, I'll up the bid, and call you with more, like, maybe even before this shit happens – but that's gonna be triple what you're paying me now, at least. Speakin' of which – tomorrow morning, when I check, there better be ten grand in that account five minutes after the bank opens, or I'm gonna give your sorry ass up to the task force cops along with your home address and the birth date of your idiot wife. Same page?"

"Yeah, yeah, it'll be there, Nook. But, you don't know my home address."

"59781 Old Hood Canal Highway."

"That's my grandparents' house, you son of a bitch! If you even think of putting that out…"

"Ok, Ping-Punk. That's good enough for me. Just think – if you don't pay me, I can stop by there, use a little evil persuasion, and get your address out of them. Hey, shit. I think you better deposit twelve grant into my account – two more, just to keep me from visiting your nice old grand-folks. Whaddya think, Pongie-Butt?"

"You mother fucker, fuck off. I'll put in ten and that's it. And if you ever threaten to harm my family again…"

"Calm down, fool. Just simmer down. Ten large will work. I'll call the bank in the morning, and as long as it's there, we've still got a working operation. But, listen, dude… You've got inside rot in your little tomato patches. That little slut that Turnip was hanging with the last few days – she was a narc."

"What!"

"Yeah, man. You know that old fish processing plant down on the beach below the caverns that got raided tonight?"

"Yeah, yeah, I know the place… it's been closed for years. The Indians bought it from the Swedes, ran it for a few years, and then shut it down – they sold all the processing equipment out of there, and now it's just like a big, old abandoned warehouse…"

"Right, that's the place. Well, local kids throw parties there now, in the summer – hell, all year long. Sheriff's have gone out once or twice and shut it down – but it's so far out there, way out on the DeWatto spit, that nobody really cares what goes down out there, unless some rich kid O.D.s or somebody gets killed, you know."

"Yeah, so what are you sayin'?"

"Well, that's where Turnip picked up that slut who turned out to be a narc for the task force. But, I'm thinking – since that whole area just got busted – that old warehouse might be cold as a witch's tit in a week or so. Shit, man – nobody's gonna party there – nobody's gone go within a mile of the place – at least not in the next week. It's still wrapped and sealed with crime-scene tape. For that matter, so are the caverns."

"Wait a minute – I heard that there was some huge, monstrous dude – like, seven feet tall and four hundred pounds – like, Bigfoot – living down in the caverns, eating people, and shit. Pumpkin told me he was bulletproof…"

"Hey, that dude is gone, man. They scooped him up in the net in tonight's bust. I heard it took six deputies to hold him, and tasers wouldn't work – they had to call in another prison van just to haul his big old ass out of there – but focus, Ping, focus. What about waiting a week or so, then, when we find out who ratted out this operation, we take 'em to the caverns, and torture 'em there?"

"You're nuts, Nooksak. Ten grand in your account tomorrow, by 10 a.m. But listen, you Indian fuck, if you ever even make the slightest suggestion threatening me or my family again, you will be dead and buried where the fucking skunks couldn't even find you in two hours time – you got me, Nook?"

"Yeah, sure, Ping. No problemo. Don't forget the ten large…"

Chiuk was talking to a dead cell phone, which he closed. He climbed back aboard the small, sleek motor sailor and quickly changed clothes. He then pulled the boat even farther up the rocky beach, and tethered it with nylon rope to a large maple tree trunk.

Dressed well, with tan slacks, Blue Canyon all-weather shoes, herringbone sport coat over a green poplin collar shirt, with a brand new brown wool short brim fedora, Chiuk Indeska stepped up onto the rocks and made his way through the woods to a small path which was undetectable if one did not know of its existence. Extremely well-worn, often trod and clean of weeds and small brush, the path led upwards through the forest to some distant lights. Lights like those that would shine from old lanterns. As Chiuk got closer to the lights, low voices could be heard, echoing through the trees. He paused in his quiet trek, stood stock-still, and listened to the voices for a minute or two. Then, with a short nod, satisfied that they were the ones he wanted to hear, he proceeded up the path into the lantern light.

Chapter 18

Franklin Opano pulled the phone earbud out and dropped it as he pulled into the driveway of his three-acre lakefront home, cruising up the driveway, then circling around to park in the waterfront garage, he thought about the conversation he had just had with his half-brother. How strange, after so many years, he was working with him again. And, how strange, that now, after all these years, the concept of what was considered "good" and what was considered "bad" moral behavior had blended into such a gray area. But, Opo know that he would not hesitate to bring the shit down in a rain of hellfire if that's what it came to.

Stepping out of his Lexus and walking into the breezeway which joined his garage to his house, his two-hundred dollar shoes crunching on the concrete, Opo reflected on the effrontery of the idiot who he'd known all his life, and who had just threatened to involve his immediate family in the turmoil and ruckus of the investigation he was involved in, in a sick, fascinating kind of way. If Spreckles knew where his extended family lived, his entire life was on the line – well, that was it. Spreckles would have to die. And if nothing changed in the next 24 hours, Franklin Opano would have to fly.

And certain other idiots would have to die.

Chapter 19

Cowboy drove up to the top of Lider Road in a medium-grade snow-storm, with about six inches on the ground and another four inches falling. At the intersection with Sidney Road, he stopped the truck, and watched the thick flakes falling through his headlights. Across the way, he looked at the words painted on the old cedar fence that he had seen for the last thirty year, still there:

"Kidnap County: Come on vacation, leave on probation"

Cowboy gave a brief, internal chuckle, gunned the truck up, and took a left turn, into the oncoming snowstorm.

Driving down Sidney Road, the ancient rural route, as the old fir forests surrounded him, driving past old Walt's Christmas Tree Farm, and the old Finnish horse farms, on into the falling snow, as he started crying, as he started wondering if it would work out, if the wife of his dreams really was the wife he thought he knew, but he would protect Hoquiam, little girl, at all costs – at all costs.

Cowboy drove on, into the snowstorm. He started to hum, then broke out into singing the words of a song that he had co-written with Nancy, called "Time and Again."

"I'm so lonely now

I think I must be the loneliest of all.

I'm so lonely now

I think the night might take my call

Because I'm lonely every day

There's no lover that comes my way

And I know that I try

To talk to passers-by

But not one gives me the time of day.

And I know that when the night falls

I'll be remembering
When the old phone called.
Why did it have to end
So hard, between a friend
And a broken heart.
Is it too late for a new lone star
and I ask myself
Time and again.
Time and again.
I'm so weary now
I'm the weariest of all.
I'm so dreamy now
I think the rain will take my call.
Because, I'm working hard every day
To earn my keep and to keep my pay
And I try to keep my eyes up to the sky
But it don't seem to give me
The time of day.
And I know when morning comes
I'll hear the sound that makes me come around
If there's a beginning again,
It starts with a friend.
So I'm not giving up
I'm gonna wait here with an open cup
Time, time, and again
Oh, yeah, I know,
Time, time, and again."

Cowboy wiped the tears off as his windshield wipers did the same to the slush and snow. He knew that losing Nancy to some endless glitter of fame was not the end of the world – he knew she was out there on her road and she deserved it; having talent was one thing, having talent and the innate sense of strength and vigor to endure endless rehearsals and hundreds of hours on the stage before a live audience was another. Talent wasted is talent untrusted.

But, basically, Cowboy was just a rural-raised and rura-thinkin' man who engendered a close-knit quality between people who raised animals on small farms, did controlled logging in the vast hill and mountains in the Olympic Peninsula, and kept a certain intersection code between whites and reservation Indians. This was a code he knew like the back of his heart, a code that he had lived by all his life, as both as a law enforcement officer and a small-time remodeling contractor. It was a code he would not break.

Upon reaching the 26-mile marker, as the snow was getting heavier, although less wet, Cowboy turned off the asphalt onto a dirt driveway flanked by two mailboxes. The one on the left was white, regulation size, and had letters on the sides which read "D.J. LIMEN". The one on the right, which was black, and stood about twelve feet off the ground (out of reach of local varmints and the rural mailmen) had letters on the sides which simply read "Bills and Pissants".

Cowboy's truck crunched up the gravel driveway as he pondered what sort of advice he was gonna ask from his oldest friend.

As his truck plowed through the snowdrifts towards the orange and yellow lights of the "Rat Lodge", Cowboy also pondered about D.J. Limen. Also know as Dr. Jay Limen, former tony/gang member from the purple (on his mom's side) and from the green (from his illustrious uncles), Jay Limen had grown into his local roots as well in his years.

He was standing in front of his barn when Cowboy came spinning up the last snowdrift, his chains barking into the ice-bitten gravel.

"So, little snow-kitten, what brings you up to my forbidden castle gates?" boomed the voice of Dr. Jayson Limen.

"It is I, dick-head, your big-dicked cousin coming up to tell you how it is and how to do it."

"Oh, yeah, okay. It's my asshole cousin, Cowboy Hat. C'mon up, Cowboy Hat. Nobody gonna shoot you. For now. Ha, ha ha, ha, ha, ha! Hey, everybody, it's my cousin Cowboy, also known as the big-time little-time remodeling contractor and part-time forest pig! That's right, my brothers – my cousin Cowboy is a cop! OK OK OK? Five-o, right here, now everybody look out!"

"Jay, shut up. Nobody cares what you say anymore. I mean – look around you. Nobody's even here, man."

Dr. Limen looked around, his head turning from side to side in a measured, even motion, and decided that he had to agree with Mr. Davenport. The layout was as it was before. Yes, Mr. Davenport?

Dr. Limen motioned to Cowboy to get out of his truck. The snow was falling heavier than it was before. The flakes were 2½ to 3 inches wide, in clusters, lit up by an almost-moonless sky – there was a new moon in the arms of the old – and the starlit wind was stirring and tossing the branches and treetops of the heavy old growth fir trees spilling hundreds of pounds of snow with each wind blow, as gigantic, snow-heavy bags of black-grey clouds huffed along in the chill breezes blowing through the treetops.

The two men went up the large, wooden stairs to the covered deck of the "Rat Lodge", stomping their boots to knock off the snow and ice. After the door into the house was opened, each sat down on small, wooden stools set just inside, and untied and removed their boots. Cowboy shrugged off his heavy sheepskin coat, hung it on a peg, and followed Dr. Limen into the kitchen. Wordlessly, Limen poured two jigger shots of Maker's Mark bourbon – which, eye to eye, they both chugged; then poured two more, which, at a nod by Limen towards the door into the enormous living room, they carried these in and took comfortable seats in leather recliner chairs set before a fire roaring in a stone-built firebox the size of everyone's fondest rural winter's dreams.

"So, what's up, doc?" rumbled the voice of Limen. "What brings you on the wings of what might turn into the heaviest snowstorm we've had, and counting? Seems to me you owed me a visit in the time of autumn, and yet I did not hear the crunch of your truck tires on the gravel of my drive. What need brings you hence, young, copper-popper?"

Cowboy rattled his thoughts, started to laugh, changed his mind, and instead replied, "Why do you talk like a cuckoo clock from the medieval ages? You know why I came. You pour Maker's Mark bourbon, you've got the best fireplace in Nipsak County, and you're always here, since you retired from hustling old retirees out of their dotage-fundage, which, I remind you, Dr. Lee-Man, I invested quite a few funds in myself over the years."

They both sipped at their bourbon, wiggled their socks at the fire, and gave a few grumps.

"Humph. Well said, little sock dragon. However, I sense an unease in your spirit. Has something gone amiss in the illustrious career of our most underrated, under-decorated, courageous and fearless part-time knight-carpenter-rock-star-husband?"

Cowboy huffed out a sigh. "Yeah, maybe. Just maybe it has, Doc. I got a call – you know I've got a spy in Nancy's tour group that has my private cell phone number – and I guess that she might be fucking around on me, out on the road. Oh, Christ, man, I just can't see her doing it – but, shit, Doc, if she is – well, I just don't know what I'm gonna do when she gets back – how I'm gonna confront her, you know?"

Cowboy chugged his bourbon and got up to get another.

"There's a beer in the fridge for you, little popsicle. But, you're done on the brown fire water. Hokay?"

Cowboy paused in the doorway. "Yeah, OK, Doc. You're right – enough calories to add to my weight. Actually, I grab a cup of your java."

"Hokay, slime-worm." Limen held out his glass. "Good thinking. But you can give me a refill since you're going that way."

Cowboy took his glass, did the drinks, and returned just as Dr. Limen was adding a log to the fire.

"Peace, and good fortune."

"Peace, and may you find it before you die."

They toasted and drank, and settled back into their chairs.

"Well, Cowboy Hat, does Nancy know about your spy? You think? I've never been in a band on a cross-country tour, but – don't the rumors fly between those band mates and their road crew? And – even if your girls don't know about your informer – how are you gonna broach the fact that you know she got laid? Are you Mr. Know-It-All, all of a sudden, out of the blue?"

"Shit, man, I don't know." Cowboy took his hat off and set it, crown down, on a side table, and ran his hand through his thick, black, graying head of hair. "And there's Hoquiam to think about."

"Yes, there is, sasquatch. But, there's you to think about, too. How much does it bother you? Would you leave her for this?"

"Well, fuck, Doc – some asshole roadie or itinerant tour-for-hire side-musician putting his dick into the treasure of my life, the only girl I've ever really loved, the mother of my daughter? Hell, I don't know how I'm gonna face her – probably just tell her the truth, that Cynthia was my spy, and told me."

"You trust this Cynthia, to not be making this shit up, to maybe get herself in with you, as in - break up with Nan and get next to you?"

Cowboy rubbed his forehead again, thinking, pondering. The logs crackled and snapped glowing sparks in the gigantic river-stone fireplace. Outside, the snow fell in heavy, white, continuous clumps.

"Hey, Doc," Cowboy suddenly said. "You know, I think I might have to spend the night. It's snowing really heaving now, and even with my four-wheel drive, I…"

"I knew that when you drove up, cheesecake, and so did you. You know where your bed is in this house, you always have. Now quit dodging the subject at hand. Do you trust this Cynthia spy-girl, or not? Your marriage, the future life of your daughter, and everything that you hold dear could be – hell, boy, is – on the line here. Who the hell is this spy of yours?"

"Well, Doc, yeah, I trust her. You see – I put her in there on the tour – and guess what, she's a cop. She's a registered reserve Nipsak County deputy, on official leave. I signed her out myself."

"Now, how the hell did you do that, young wonder-fuck? Being as the fact that you're nothing more than a reserve patrol officer yourself, with not that many years in, I might add?"

"Not anymore, Doc. I'm a fully vested member of the department, rank of investigative sergeant, on call in the field, Narcotics, with additional appointments working interactive ongoing investigations with a special task force. Big Tom brought me in, along with Chief Bigelow and Franklin Opano from the Navy."

Dr. Limen slammed his recliner forward so hard he spilled the his drink, setting his thick socks on the carpet, and leaned forward, peering at Cowboy with a glare as intense as the flames in the fireplace.

"Who? Who, man? Who the fuck did you say, that last name you said? Say it again, now! Say it again, I say, greenwood!"

"What?" Cowboy was totally taken aback by his friend's outburst. "Who? You mean uh – Franklin Opano?"

"Franklin Opano. Holy shit falling on a golden field of poppy plants in a field in Afghanistan. Franklin Opano. Damn, damn, and hot damn mama. That's the name, alright. Franklin Opano." Dr. Limen leaned back in his chair, easing off the tension in the room, as Cowboy looked at him in obvious wonder. The good doctor was now rubbing his gnarled hands over his own corrugated brow.

"What, Doc? What the hell is the fucking deal, here? Between my dad, Chief Bigelow, and now you, the fucking reactions and shit involving this guy – what the hell is it?"

Limen eyed Cowboy carefully. "Let me ask you something, young Nipsak knave. Does this have something to do with a half-Suquamish tribal member named Chiuk Al-Indeska, also known as Spreckles, who used to work for the reservation fisheries county, counting humpies, smolts, and sockeye spawn? Further – does it have anything to do with Big Tom and Nancy? Further, little eaglet, just what exactly does this investigation hope to accomplish?"

Cowboy eyeballed the doctor right back. "Those are heavy questions, Lime Man. You, of all people, know that as a sworn officer I cannot divulge information regarding anyone or anything in an ongoing, active criminal investigation – even if I wanted to, now, and even if you weren't a retired officer yourself. I will tell you this much, against, my better judgement." Cowboy ran his own recliner forward, so his socks hit the carpet, and stared down his older friend. "In a word, Doc – yes."

Limen leaned his head back and threw out a heavy sigh. "I thought so, skilled hunter. I thought so. And now, it becomes a little clearer why you, my oldest friend and student, sit here in the place we always called the Rat Lodge. I had a feeling, when I heard your tired crunching up the gravel and ice of my driveway this evening. Yes, I had a feeling. And as you well know – in your own words, you of all people should know – my intuitive feelings are not to be taken lightly."

"Of course, Doc. It's why you got fired off the force."

"Not fired, eaglet. Simply passed over for promotion, and retired. Put out to seed, so to speak."

"Whatever, Doc. Now, explain what the fuck is the meaning of all this shit about Spreckles?"

"How much do you know?"

"You know I can't divulge information regarding..."

"Fuck that!" roared Dr. Limen. "How much do you know?"

"We tracked Spreckles to a drug lab out in the hills above DeWatto, out off the lost highway. We had agents in there – we had him pinned down, and he got away."

"He will always get away."

Chapter 20

Standing together, in a clearing far out in the woods, Cowboy nuzzled the wonderfully scented, soft neck of his chief deputy, Cynthia. As far out from town as they were, the full moon refracting on one side of the sky was dancing its glowing light off the deep green shadows of the towering firs, blue spruces, and orange madrona of the forest. Pol-tee-ahn-nee-a-ska-iu – moonlight in the tree tops. And on the other side, in a light-blue shading to the deepest-lit blue, the stars were sparkling green, orange, yellow, red, and blue fire. Coyotes sung in the distance, along with some dogs on the outskirts. Hard to believe, if you've spent your life in the city, but it's out there – especially on Indian reservations. Until the gigantic lights of the casinos, that is – glowing 24 hours a day. (Something for everybody.)

Cowboy used to go to a clearing, four miles from town to see this. Now it was forty miles.

He nuzzled Cynthia's neck again, trying to draw her gorgeous mouth around for a deep, starlit kiss.

"Hey, starfucker. What about your kid? Don't you have to go and pick up Hoqi pretty soon?" she asked. She stayed in his arms, however, her back pressed against his front as they stared up at the brilliant sky show, sweat still dampening their uniforms, which were hastily and sloppily put back on after their starglow ground fuck.

"Nah, baby – she's almost eighteen years old. I know what she's doing with old Henry's kid, out there behind that shack – and so do you."

"And what about Nancy?"

"Ah, Christ, Cynthia. Nancy's in another world now, fuck, man, she's got three hit songs, her CDs are selling above the charts, they can't press 'em fast enough. They're talking about her playing the lead in a Hollywood film, I don't know if she's in Paris, Africa, or London at this point. And I don't care."

She squeezed his leg. "I know that you still love her."

"I'll always love her, Cyn, she's the mother of my daughter. But all the rest is just memories from ancient times, and this is here and now, baby…"

Cynthia squirmed out of his grasp, and whirled around to face him, eyes blazing. She thumped her fists on his chest, looking up at him. "Cowboy, would you have a child with me? Will you marry me?"

"Of course, Cyn, as soon as we can get through a divorce…"

Cowboy's collar mic chirped. "7-9, 7-9."

Cowboy keyed his mic. "This is 7-9."

"Yes – disturbance in trailer park, located rover patrol, advise, over."

"Ok, patch rover to me, over."

"7-9, 1411, Deputy Alandra. We have an escalating 2-11 at Relmer Trailer courts, have called backup. Request sergeant on scene."

"1411, sergeant will respond. Field advisory to other rovers for back-up."

Cowboy looked at Cynthia, shrugged, and said, "You better get going."

"I'm the rover sergeant tonight? I thought it was Big Ben…"

"Big Ben is busy in south county, darling. Keeping an eye on that endless frac-lab shit still going on. You go, I'll follow – call me in if anything heavy happens. Otherwise – I've done my time on these DVs. It's your turn, Cyn. Just remember…"

"Yeah, I know, mushy. DVs are the worst – the liverwurst – the calls where most of us get involved in the worst way. Kiss me, and I'll see you in hell."

Cowboy did that. As she rapidly walked to her cruiser, parked on the edge of the magical clearing, he watched her adjust the back of her shoulder weapons rig – just like any patrol deputy would do. The he keyed his mic again. "1411, 10-20."

"Edge of park, 7-9. Initial responding team is investigating – we've got two exits from this place. I'm on east, 1299 is on west."

"Ok, nature of call."

"Wife-beater, been there before – he's crazy when he's drunk."

"Ok, sergeant on the way. I'll be command rover. A lot of these dudes have heavy friends who follow our scanners, so switch freqs now to my call – coyote simple – you got that, 1411?"

"Got it, coyote simple, understood. Responding team switching frequency."

There was a pause on the airwaves as the radios switched to a secure channel which blocked civilian scanners. Then cowboy keyed back in on the new freq. "1411, give me a sit-rep. We're secure."

"Waiting for the lights of your rover, Lieutenant. Responding officers are surrounding the trailer in question – neighbors' calls continuing to come in to 911, advising yelling, screaming, breaking glass. Now, we've got a report of gunshots."

"1411, do you have backup units deployed on park exits?"

"Park exits are blocked, 7-9."

"1411…"

"7-9, I've got a medium size pickup truck, dark blue, moving at rapid, dodging erratic, park speed bumps – yeah – he's heading across the big open meadow on the east end of the park, heading for the east exit…"

"Block it. Use all backup."

"Exit blocked, military style?"

"Affirmative, affirmative, all units block east exit – rover sergeant, Cynthia, do you copy?"

"Two minutes out, lieutenant, just coming down the road."

"All right, now listen, Cyn. I think perps, blue pickup, east side. Let sit and cover that. Cover west side, watch for perps' friends – they're runners, Cyn – armed and 9-16, you copy?"

"Copy, armed and warrants, affirmative. Any thoughts of a sky boy?"

"Good idea, if we can get one up in time. Block west exit, Cyn, arms out and take control. Out." Cowboy keyed outside mic. "This is D.S. Nipsak Lieutenant Davis Cowboy Mooney field command, dispatch direct on emergency sky monitor rover 2-19 – request eye-in-the-sky; I'm monitoring emergency sit-rep of shots fired, possible fleeing felons, blue pickup truck, medium size, heading out of Relmert Trailer Park, east entrance – spotlight – once again – illumination on medium size blue pickup truck – follow suspects as they leave east entrance, spot and nail for ground units to apprehend – consider code 16."

Suddenly Cynthia's calm voice came over the air. "7-9, I've got the blue pickup coming out of the west entrance, he's coming right at me – shots fired, passenger side. Evading – hold on."

"1490, run hot now, and forward yourself out. You've got backup, run hot pursuit."

"Roger that, 7-9."

"7-9, we've got him, he's headed toward highway 16 – in pursuit."

"We've got him blocked – when he comes over the hill before Mullenix. Units 14-x – block him out."

"Already got him, 7-9 – he hit the ditch and Andrews and Fengyle got him at gunpoint."

There was a pause. "Ok – original responding officers take statements – I want one unit to stay on site on backup on that, and… rover sergeant?"

"Rover sergeant."

"Take command of hook up and load…"

"Already done, Lieutenant. Suspect in custody, disarmed and hooked up."

"Ok, team units, real good work, stand down from this one, your rover commander will cover your event reports. 1411?"

"1411, sir, go ahead."

"Outstanding, 1411. Good response time. Fill out your radio and head to the barn."

"Thanks, 7-9. Responding."

"1490?"

"1490, on recall."

"1490, cover 1411's shift, two more hours, copy? I've got you for fill in."

"No problem, Lieutenant. We like night work."

"Ok – zero out at 0400 hours. Good heads up. File your reports and I'll review. You know I'm your sarge."

"Thanks, Lieutenant."

"No problem. Have a good shift."

"Have a good shift."

"No problem."

"Thanks, Philo."

"Sorry that we were a little late on backup."

"Nobody is late on backup, Smith – you got there as soon as you could. Don't worry about it."

"5-9, in the can."

"7-9 – out for the count. The night shift command will be passed onto daylight Lieutenant Bielson, at 0600 hours. Let it be duly noted in the log book of the night desk command of Nipsak County that good old Cowboy is signing off – once again, rover sergeant, outstanding cover on the backside of that gate."

"That's a roger, sir – backup much appreciated for apprehension."

"7-9 going 10-40 out."

"7-9 going 10-40 and off the air, have fun boys and girls, see you next shift."

Just as Cowboy was taking off his duty belt and heading back to the car, about to head to the barn, his radio crackled with the cool, collected voice of the dispatcher. Oh shit, he thought.

"7-9, 7-9, shift commander, we have an incident call from 911, a probably 287 – repeat – 287, violent homicide possible off Fragaria Road in Olalla – neighbors report perps firing, repeat, gunshots fired, hold."

Cowboy adjusted his waist belt so that his taser holster, gun holster, handcuff slip and ammunition canister release were more comfortable and gunned his unit down the road. It was 5:47 a.m. He was tired, the whole shift was tired. It was perfect. These calls came in and demanded immediate response. It was what they lived for.

"7-9 to rover sergeant. Back on line, Cyn. Move it."

"Right behind you. Ready for field command."

"7-9, dispatch. Proceed to intersection of Olalla Valley Road and Crystal Point, and hold for backup."

"This is rover sergeant. I've got incoming shots fired, I'm taking hits on my vehicle, going into spinout on Banner Road, repeat, request…"

It was Cynthia. Cowboy rocketed his cruiser into a turn around and wailed up Prospero Road to Fragaria Landing.

"7-9 to rover, respond."

"Rover in deep shit, 7-9. Spinning out, trying to evade heavy incoming fire…"

Then all Cowboy could hear was bullets smacking metal. And then a smashing sound — after which the communication from his rover sergeant went dead.

"7-9, all units – co-respond to rover sergeant – backups move in now, now, now."

"1411, I've got her, Lieutenant, she's okay."

"1490, I've just jammed down the west side backup, Lieutenant – you have to come up and see this, sir."

"Your 20 is?"

"Old Orchard Road and Washout Point."

"I'm there, I'm four-out."

Cowboy drove up to the dented cruiser in the darkness. He lit up 1490 with his side-lights, and spotted the sheriff's deputy, obviously shaken, standing by the road. 1490 was a mid-patrol veteran, four years out of the academy. As Cowboy stopped his cruiser and got out to stand on the road beside him, the deputy slumped his shoulders and held out his hand. In it was a note, written on thick yellow paper.

Cowboy patted the deputy on the shoulder, suggested he get back in his own cruiser for further instructions, and then clicked on his Maglite for a look at the note that he held in his hand.

"Spreckles used all his lives," it said. Cowboy turned the page over. "Spreckles ain't my name. And Cowboy ain't your name either. Son of Manta, friend. More to follow. Take care of Thistlebone and Bird-Wing tribe – all will be revealed soon. Talk to George. Watch your back. Follow bear tracks to bear traps. Beware of messages from Indians off tribal land. Signed, Chiuk."

Cowboy stood there, turning the message over and over, as his collar mic and unit mic chirped with incoming messages.

"7-9, this is rover sergeant, I'm okay."

"7-9 – that dude got away, man – wait a minute, homes – is that you, my old brother?"

Cowboy keyed his mic. "Chiuk Al-Indeska, is that you talking, is that you, Chiuk, over?"

"Yeah, Cowboy. Hey, ya-tah-hey, long time, huh?"

"Chiuk, how is it that you're on this frequency?"

"Cowboy, you know me – I'm intertribal – I can communicate on all call bands, at all times, and I'll tell you something else, son of Tom…"

"No, I'll tell you something else, Chiuk Al-Desk-Ah. It has been many years since the Suquamish Tribe has wished to have you sit down with us in elder council and come forward with the confession that we need to hear. Since I sit on that council now, I can tell you that the worst that will happen is that I will take you in to the sheriff's office for questioning."

"Oh, really, is that right, little Tom? Son of Big Tom? Listen, brother – and you are my brother – I know how you got the nickname Cowboy, just like you know how I got the nickname Spreckles. I used to stick my snout into the sugar bowl, and you used to love to walk around in a cowboy hat. But guess what, young elder. I've got to sign off – but, talk to Mr. Limen, and talk to your dad, Big Tom Mooney, and talk to the man who taught us how to move boulders – we're still on the same side, brother Cowboy. Don't worry about your rover sergeant, Cyn's okay. And don't worry about Chief Bigelow. And, you know what else, humpie? Don't worry about spawning in the creek that nurtured you as a Suquamish Salmon Indian, because I've got that covered, too – endangered that you are.

"I've got to go now. I love you, Cowboy. And I know you loved my sister. But, she is gone – far away from you now. It's better that you are with Cynthia, okay Cowboy. I'll talk to you later."

There was a click, then silence.

"Wait! Dispatch!"

"Yes, 7-9. We've got you."

"How was it that guy could patch in like that?"

"Not sure, sir. We're checking it out. We're backtracking his inline code, but so far, it's a deadline trail, Lieutenant."

"Well, keep trying, trace it down. He talked to me for a good 80 seconds, on a closed, secure, private law enforcement line. I thought we had FBI briefing on that. And where the hell is my rover sergeant, by the way? And 1411, and 1490, everybody on that okay?"

"1411, ok, Lou."

"1490, ok, Lou. We're wrapped."

"Ok. Rover sergeant?"

"Rover sergeant ok, Lou. Just a little bumped up after that last chase. I'm with the medics now. Ok if I take off early shift?"

"No problem, rover. Once again, out – standing work tonight."

"Thanks, Lou. See you tomorrow."

"1411?"

"Here, Lou."

"Did you hear that last transcommunication between myself and the possible perpetrator?"

"Every word, Lou, and so did dispatch. We've got it all down on tape."

"Ok, good. Now, let's head to the barn, turn over the watch command, and get some sleep. We'll try to figure this crap out tomorrow. Ok, Corporal Wiley?"

"Ok, sir. Glad we got to hook up some crooks on this shift."

"Me too, Wiley. Talk to you tomorrow. Let's go over the transcript of that dispatch tape at command center, and see what we can come up with."

"Sounds good, sir."

"Corporal Wiley?"

"Yes, sir."

"You don't have to call me sir."

"But – you're a lieutenant now, sir."

"Oh, yeah, that's right. Corporal Wiley?"

"Yes, sir."

"Switch to cell phone."

"We're off the air."

"As of tomorrow, you are a sergeant, ok?"

"Whatever you say, sir."

"Corporal Wiley?"

"Yes, sir?"

"I'm making you a sergeant so that you won't call me sir no more. I mean, anymore. Ok? Sergeant Wiley?"

"Uh, ok, sir. Sir?"

"What, Sergeant Wiley?"

"Do I get more pay now, with the sergeant's rank?"

"Yes, you do, Sergeant Wiley."

"Sir?"

"Hey, man…"

"Uh, I mean – Lieutenant?"

"Call me Lou, Sergeant Wiley."

"Uh, oh, yeah, right, ok. Lou?"

"Yes, sergeant."

"How much more?"

"About 20%, sergeant."

"No shit?"

"No shit."

"So, sir – I mean, Lou – how come I got this promotion? With more pay and all?"

"To bring up your brain cells, sergeant. I need fresh brain cells."

"Oh, yeah. I get it. With that pay raise, I'm smarter already, Lou."

"Hey, Sergeant Wiley?"

"Yeah, Lou?"

"Only senior homicide detectives and inspectors get to call me Lou. To you, it's still lieutenant, ok, sergeant?"

"Oh, yeah. Sure, Lou. I mean, lieutenant. Sorry, I forgot."

"That's alright, sergeant. Now, go and open the car door for the day captain, before he slips on the ice and breaks his hip."

"Right, Lou. Right away. I'm on it."

"Ok, good. I'm going to go back to the barn, light a cigar, and see if I can figure out the shift report of the last fourteen hours. No calls, sergeant."

"Right, Lou. No calls."

"Good. Out."

<h1 style="text-align:center">Chapter 21</h1>

Nancy, who weighed in at a hefty 185 pounds now, sat across from her daughter Hoquiam, who was a slim 120, and Hoqi"s fiancé, who was about her mother's weight. All very confusing. Nancy remembered when she weighed 120, and Hoqi – 20.

"Well, Mom," began Hoquiam, who was quickly silenced by her mother.

"Wiley – I guess it's Sergeant Wiley now, is it?"

The fellow sitting next to Hoqi on the couch nodded, squeezing her hand. Hoqi squeezed back and smiled.

"Yes, ma'am. I got promoted last week by your husband, Lieutenant Mooney, after a fierce night of work on Mullenix Ridge…"

"Yeah, I know, sergeant. And please don't call me ma'am. For that matter, since I outrank you in years, I won't call you sergeant. What's your full name, Wiley?"

"Theodore James Wiley, ma'am. I mean, Mrs. Cowboy. I mean, Mrs. Mooney. I mean, uh…"

The sound of sudden, delighted female laughter rang through the room, ringing like chimes in harmony, as mother and daughter reveled in the young man's discomfiture and obvious sincerity. How could you not love this kid, thought Nancy, a little wistfully. She then grew serious, and turned her level gaze on her daughter.

"You know what it's like, being married to a cop. It's almost like being married to every criminal in Nipsak County. I can't tell you how many times I waited up for Cowboy…"

"And he waited up for you, mom, coming home late, or not at all, from road tours… The 'Gruesome Ransom' tour, the 'Popular Diety' tour, the 'Miraculous Indian Rising' tour, the…"

"Alright, On-hola-esk. Quit naming all my CD titles."

"Well, your tours were named after them, Mom, and I grew up hearing those names when I'd ask Daddy where you were, when you would be coming back home to stay with us – for a little while, until he next one would whisk you off to New Zealand, Japan, Europe, or, my favorite, the 'Fakey-Hoqi-Karaoke' tour…"

"Yeah, okay. I thought you liked that I named that CD after you."

"Fakey-Hoqi-Karaoke? C'mon, man. That's a fucking insult."

"HOQUIAM!" Both mother and fiancé looked at the composed young lady in semi-horror and faked movie shock.

"Alright, ok, sorry. Anyway, Mom – me and Wiley want to have the wedding next month, here on the reservation."

Nancy looked at the groom-to-be. She groomed him with her eyes. He grunted, fidgeted, and finally said, "Uh, yeah, Mrs…"

"Call me Nancy, Theodore. By the way – do you like my music?"

"Sure do, ma'am. I've got 'Dancing with the Animals' and 'Frivolous Afterthoughts' on my rapid play carousel in my car. Also 'Nick's Last Timepiece'. I think that's my favorite. I…"

"Ok, stop," intoned Hoqiuam. "I don't want to talk about your music, Mom. That's not what this is about."

A sudden breeze blew through the open French doors, fragrant with balsam from the enormous forest next to the house. The hissing of a Chiulk-na'tonda, rain falling through the trees, quickly followed. It remained fairly warm and pleasant, however. In late April, it looked like it would be an early spring. The three of them sat there, listening. Hoquiam's eyes glistened with pleasure, mirroring those of her mother.

"Wiley. Do you have Indian blood?"

"About one third, ma'am. Snohomish mostly. Some Puyallup and Tukwila. You know how people around there mix it up…"

Nancy grinned, leaned forward, got a Sherman MCD light out of the pack on the low-rise coffee table, and lit a cigarette.

"Mom, when are you gonna stop smoking?" nagged her daughter. "Just because you're fucking that stupid roadie who looks like an ape and smokes like a factory doesn't mean…"

"Shut up, Hoqi."

"...doesn't mean you have to," she finished defiantly. Hoqi glared at her rock star mother. "And it doesn't mean you have to get fat like him, either, which you are, by the way. Also – he smells like fish. Why is that?"

"Well, my dear one, that you should be able to figure out by yourself. You two kind of smell like fish, too, right now. What have you been doing recently? Before you came over here, for instance?"

Furious blushing commenced from Theodore, and giggling from Hoquiam.

"Touché, Mother. Well played. Now will you put that fucking cigarette out so we can talk about the wedding?"

"No, Hoquiam, I won't. As a matter of fact, I think a glass of wine is in order. Will you have one, Theodore? Or perhaps you'd like something stronger – I think I've got some whiskey lying around in the cupboard – or, since you're not in uniform, sergeant, how about we spark up a joint? I've got some killer stuff..."

"Mother!" yelled Hoquiam. "Stop it! Wiley's got something to say to you, anyway."

"Well, ma'am, I mean, Nancy..." Wiley firmed up his confidence and looked Nancy straight in the eyes. "Since Hoqi and me are gonna get married – I thought I'd quit the Nipsak County force and join the Suquamish Tribal Police. You know, less heavy crime, less call outs..."

"Yes, young one. And, lest we forget, less pay, less chance of promotion, more chance of chasing down drunk drivers coming out of the casinos..." Nancy paused, and regarded Wiley with a heavy lidded look. "Are you a chicken eater, Theodore?"

"Oh, you bet, ma'am. I..."

"Mother, stop it."

"Stop what, my little sunflower? Doesn't she look just like a little sunflower when she's angry, sergeant? Face black in the middle, full of little seeds of frustration, and all yellow flower petals wilting on her cheeks, blossoming rage through those edges of her dark hair and dew-dropped eyelashes..."

"Ok, Mom, that's it. We're leaving." Hoquiam started to rise up off the couch.

"No, wait a minute, Hoqi. I got this one." Wiley gave Nancy the full strength of his glance. "Listen, I know who you are – now getting up there age-wise, senior tribal royalty, all that. And I do listen to your CDs. And they get me off, lady. I really can get next to your music. But, do me one little favor, as a mom, as my future mother-in-law, and quit baiting me, watching me rise up to it – and quit fucking with my wife, ok? Can you do that, Nancy Thistlebone? Just one time? Let's watch, and see if these words change your outlook on this part of your family that you're facing now."

Both mother and daughter stared with wide eyes at the sudden young warrior in their midst. The rain outside fell a bit heavier for a moment, and then subsided. There was even more forest balsam in the breeze which wafted through the room – but this time, it had a distinctly masculine tang to it – an edge of earthiness, a natural pride.

"Well, Hoquiam. I am impressed. Yes, most impressed. Mr. Wiley, I hereby welcome you with all my heart into our family. I warn you, however, when the wedding party gathers, people will gasp and flail when they see the fireworks that go off when I show up with my animal roadie ape-lover..." A glance at Hoquiam. "And Cowbobboy showing up with that little deputy slut on his arm. Other than that – yes, let us go forward, children."

Nancy rose up and walked over to where they were sitting, as they also got to their feet, arms around each other, and faced her.

"Oh, Mom. You're crazy, and I love you."

The hug that ensued was long, warm, and a little hurried with tears and testosterone. Some estrogen, too, was now smiling in the room's breezes.

"God," sniffed Nancy. "I swear, Teddy Boy, if I was ten years younger, I'd steal you away from her..."

"Mother, stop. And his name's not Teddy."

"Oh, that's ok, baby." Wiley drew back, with his eyes straight into Nancy's, then leaned forward and kissed her quickly. "I think we understand each other."

"By the way, Theodore, which part of the chicken bird is your favorite to eat?"

"Drumsticks, ma'am. Fine drumsticks. And also – the thighs."

"And why would that be?"

"Well, the wings ain't got much flesh on 'em – chickens rarely fly, the breasts usually got too much fat – all that skin – and the drumsticks and the thighs, well – that's what chickens use to run with, isn't it?"

Nancy's laughter was long and loud, echoing out the windows and doors of the old, wooden reservation house, finally dissolving into the mist drifting through the trees from the heavy early spring rain.

Chapter 22

Music was playing, drifting through the trees – an elusive melody that came and went, as Big Tom Mooney drove up the curving gravel road, his hairy reddish-brown arm resting on the window sill of his truck, basking in the warmth of the early summer morning.

The tune became clearer, then finally distinct as he pulled into Dr. Limen's driveway, facing the house.

"Don't you fight me
Because I'll fight you back,
You'll see we can do this
As long as the ocean is the sea
All you've got to know about living with me
The wind will teach you how to be free
But baby,
I know you will find us
If you'd just take a look inside
And get down upon your knees –
Because you know with me,
Kindness is the key."

It was a song off Thistlebone's second CD, "The Popular Deity". Big Tom smiled, yawned, cut the engine, and, without getting out of the truck, hollered, "Limen, rymen, stupid crazy pieman!" Then he lit a cigarette, leaned back in his seat, and waited.

An incredibly ancient, grey, grizzled black Labrador dog wandered up and sniffed at the truck.

"Good God, Klones, is that you?"

The dog raised his head, and blinked at the voice he recognized. His eyes were fogged over – he was quite blind. He licked his chops, and his tail began a slow, arrhythmic wag. He dropped open his mouth and smiled, tentatively.

"My God, boy – you must be about 15 years old. I thought you died years ago."

"He's fourteen, to be exact, Manta-Ray. And that's 98 in dog years. And, I'd say, all things considered, you and him look about the same." Dr. Limen came around from the back of Tom's truck, and wacked him on the arm.

"And I could say the same about you, asshole," responded Tom.

"You haven't driven up this path in at least a thousand years, Old Manta."

Tom huffed out smoke, opened the door, which creaked like a grumpy hyena, and stumped his boots onto the gravel, adjusted the weight of his 250 pounds as his gut heaved into position over the old silver rodeo buckle which kept his belt on.

"Jesus, Limen. I'm a busy man. Ain't got time for frivolous things like coming around here and visiting the likes of you, old salt."

They grinned fiercely at each other, and shook hands.

"Come in and set a spell, old pard. Up for a tiny dram, a taste of the old brown glory?"

"Shit, hombre. Does the pope run away when the bear shits in the woods?"

"Only if his pants are down, Tullio. Come on, Klones, let's take this Manta-Ray inside."

The ancient dog, who was, indeed, the son of Bones, followed them up the gigantic wooden steps of the forever-standing deck, built when Christ was a poverty-stricken, benevolent king, who wore a crown of thorns and truly cared for the homeless and afflicted. A different era, indeed, and one which did not last long. But, then again – no one can remain the same all their life.

Big Tom eased himself into the one of the leather recliners, sighing in satisfaction much like his son had, years before.

"What'll it be, old man? Maker's Mark on the rocks, or Maker's Mark straight up?"

"Just like it comes from the bottle, A-ohl-koska. Just like it pours," replied the whale, beached as he was in the house of one of the oldest friends of his family – not to speak of the fact that Dr. Limen was the half-brother of Big Deb, the woman he was married the longest to, the mother of his son, and the horsewhip of his soul. Who can get more home than that?

Dr. Limen came in, followed by the old, smelly dog, carrying a tray with drinks, crackers, and cheese. The dog flopped down at the foot of Tom's chair.

"Hey, Limen."

"What?"

"Does anybody ever snap forward in these things, and catch an animal sleeping down there? I know you got a bunch of cats around here, too. That ever happen?"

"Only once, Manta-Ray."

"And?"

"Well, the little critter lived, but never walked quite the same. Drink up, old fool."

They toasted, raising their glasses in silence, then quaffing down the golden, warm liquor.

"Ah, shit," said Tom. "I wish this moment could last forever. But, unfortunately, it can't."

"No? Why not?"

"Well, I've got some bad news, some medium-heavy bad news, some downright shitty news, some not-so-bad news, and a little bit of good news. Which do you want first?"

The good doctor settled back in his own recliner, and considered.

"Well, shit, Mooney. Since I probably already know just about everything you're gonna tell me, how about if I just tell you first? Let's start off with the bad news, and get rid of the heavy shit a little later. The air stays cleaner that way, considering the implications and the filth we're about to fling on people who are ancient family and friends."

Big Tom eyed him, owlishly. "Did I ever tell you about the time that in one five-day span, Cowboy saw five owls, five Subaru station wagons, and five..."

"Stop, Manta-Ray. There's no getting out of this one. That's why you're here."

"Ok, ok, Doc." Tom shifted his bulk. "One more drink, then, and let's get started."

112

"You know where it is – get it yourself."

Tom sighed. "Oh, well, fuck. Maybe just a cup of coffee."

"You know where it is, get it your…"

"Ok, ok. Let's get on with it. Tell me the bad news that I was gonna tell you."

"Ok, Manta-Ray. I'll start it off with a question: since you've been in the music business for thirty years, more or less – can you think of a more terrifying moment than being a world renowned recording artist, a true star in your field of performing your original music on stage before thousands of people, and falling completely apart while on tour?"

"Doc – that was going to be my middle-heavyweight news. Nancy is done – that's obvious. The 'Juggling Kangaroos' tour is finished, almost before it started, and her company owes hundreds of thousands in corporate sponsor losses and pres-sold ticket refunds…"

"Yeah, I know. And it could bleed some heavy-duty nasty shit into our little out-of-the-way corner of the world, here."

"Right."

"Ok, Manta, here's the knocker – Spreckles can be contacted."

"Spreckles is dead."

"Only in the guise in which you knew him, Tom. No, Spreckles – Chiuk-Al-Indesa-Se – is very much alive. Want me to prove it?"

Tom gave a wave of his big paw. "Sure, doc. Prove away."

"Sure you don't want another drink first, Manta-Ray?"

Big Tom grumbled, shifting his weight in the recliner, then suddenly swung his huge, leonine head to stare at Dr. Limen. "What the hell you got up your sleeve, you old coot?"

Limen stared back, eye to eye with Tom, then shifted his eyes. "Chiuk Al-Deska-Se, come on out and show yourself to your old tribal member, Investigator Mooney, if you would, please."

Big Tom froze – the old dog lifted his head – the warm, summer air wafting through the room became like bubbles in a freezing fog, as footsteps were heard coming down the hallway, and a gaunt, wiry, yet strangely vibrant face appeared out of the gloom – a face from the past, etched with horrible turmoil, etched with undaunted diligence, etched with the hardness of mahogany, etched with sorrow and interminable years of loneliness, etched with the rigid, set look of a Suquamish Indian tribal elder, etched with hope and even a glimmer of warmth and humor as the eyes of a falcon drifted down to meet Tom's own.

Chiuk stopped a few feet away from Tom's recliner, looking down at him with gentle empathy. "Hey, Manta-Ray. It's good to see you. How's the fishing lately?"

Big Tom Mooney had a flashback, at that instant, of the first time that he had heard Nancy Thistlebone sing, and an epiphany rose up in his soul. "You're Nancy's brother! You're her other side!"

"Yeah, man. I am. But – I'm tired. Can I sit down, and maybe have a taste of that Maker's Mark? I could use it, right now."

"You know where it is, get it yourself," intoned Dr. Limen.

"Ok." An obviously fatigued Chiuk shuffled into the kitchen, came back with a double-full glass of the bourbon, sank into the couch, and fingered a piece of cheese off the tray. The old dog grumbled up, waddled over, and plopped down at his feet.

"He likes you."

"No, Tom – he loves me. He was my dog, before I left him with the good doctor, here – just like Bones was, before him."

"Nope. Wrong there, Spreckles. Bones was my son's dog, passed on to Hoqi when she was a little kid."

"And how did your Cowboy son come upon Bones, Manta?"

"Well, he found him by the driveway one evening, sitting next to a propped-up, cardboard sign that said 'Free Dog'."

"Yes. I always knew Cowboy could never resist anything free."

"Same with you, Chiuk. You've been off the radar scope for quite some time, until recently."

Chiuk drank deep, actually draining his glass, which he set down gently on the coffee table, after snapping a few cats out of the way. They ran off, growling and meowing, tails held high. They obviously knew him, too.

"So, this is where you've been hiding out, all this time," said Tom, ominously eyeballing Dr. Limen. "A fugitive with felony warrants, aiding and abetting – Limen, you've got one minute – exactly 60 seconds – to tell me why I shouldn't call in my son and his warrants team."

"Actually, Big Tom – I will have that second drink with you. And pour another for my esteemed friend here, who has done more to keep his people from going to the Bad Spirit Place than you or I have in our entire careers put together."

Mooney goggled at Limen. "What? Explain."

"I'll let this tired young man do that. I'll just get those drinks, and put some steaks on to broil, with that special sauce everybody likes so much. Shut up and listen to Chiuk, ok, Manta-Ray? And – quit trying to be such a macho cop. Nobody's going anywhere until this story is finished, anyway. Kloons, you stay with Chiuk – your rightful owner."

Kloons blinked – he knew the word "steaks" and had started to rise to follow Limen – but at his command, lay back down at the foot of the long-sought fugitive.

Big Tom frowned at Chiuk. "Ok, Spreckles – let's hear what the fuck you've got to say. You've got five minutes."

The figure at the end of the twenty-foot long couch, draped majestically with priceless Indian wool blankets, turned his head to solemnly regard the old cop-turned-music agent.

"And before you start – why do you look so tired, kid? Christ, you can't be much more than Nancy's age – maybe three years – and she's about, what, 47, 48? Shit, man, you look like you're 60. At least."

"Well, Manta-Ray, I've been moving boulders. Heavy stones. You know who taught me to do that, don't you?"

"Yeah. I ran into him at that DeWatto cave action with Cowboy. Where you got away."

"Yes, that's right. I thought I heard your voice booming, blathering, yelling useless commands inside that sacred cavern. That place was powerful to the local tribes that originally lived there – a thousand years ago. There are still links if you can speak the language that frees the spirit to proceed with those links – but, a big lummox like you wouldn't know. Although, you are a great music scout. You discovered my sister – just after Charlene beat you to it."

Big Tom bristled. Chiuk waved a treaty hand. "Hey, man, you know it's cool. None of us, including Mom, gave Thistle the recognition she should have had. Anyway, I had help moving those boulders that night. And – there weren't many to move – just small ones, anyway.

There was another, deeper passage there in the big rocks of that cavern – another tunnel. You, Cowboy, Peterson, the others – you would have found it, eventually, if you hadn't been distracted by the crazy laughter and rantings of our old friend, who I call the Big Pumpkin, and who you call someone else."

Big Tom bristled again. Again, the treaty hand, palm up, from Chiuk. "It's an old trick, Manta. You and Bigelow taught it to us down on the beach. Now – please, listen."

Dr. Limen brought in a tray, set it down with fresh drinks, and turned to go back to the kitchen. Mr. Kloon's eyes followed him, full of steak tidbits, and Limen intoned: "Not yet, Mr. Kloons. Your true owner is here, and he will feed you when he is ready. Now, listen, too many things of tribal and civilian importance."

Mr. Kloons nodded, and laid his head back on top of his old, grey paws. Limen stirred the fire in the gigantic hearth, and dropped in another log of seasoned maple wood, as Chiuk Al-Desk-eh finally unleashed his story to one he knew he could trust, finally, sitting in a place where he knew he was safe – among animals and men that he knew and trusted.

Chapter 23

Chiuk began: "The man whom you know as Opano Franklin, or, Franklin Opano, Lieutenant Commander in the United States Navy, is neither one of those. He is not the Opano Nancy knew from her early years; that man is dead. And – he is not a naval officer. He is an absolute imposter, in every way. He represents neither the Suquamish Tribe, nor any blood tie to Thistlebone, nor any branch of the Armed Services of the United States."

Big Tom bristled a third time. "No way, Spreckles. I was in a meeting in the federal building in Seattle – full of DEA agents, feds, cops, women lawyers, governments, the whole nine. Nobody was fake there. We had to prove security clearance just to get past the lobby, again at the elevator, and again at the 11th floor where the meeting was – hell, you can't fake that. The whole fucking building was secure. There were armed Marines walking around, for Christ's sake." Tom's face was lit up like a pumpkin on Halloween; he was leaning forward and speaking so intently at Chiuk that Old Kloons lifted his head off his paws and growled.

"No, Manta-Ray. It was fake. You were set up from that very night twenty years ago on Big Deb's deck, meeting Opo just after you'd first heard Nancy sing."

If Tom was a spring bullfrog, his head could not have bulged any larger. "Then how – what – and how could they fake that? And – what about Chief Bigelow? He was the reason I believed Opo when we had that meeting on the deck, outside the 'Low Tide' – oh, shit, man, wait a minute. I remember, I remember, I remember now like it was yesterday. Big Deb was warning me, warning me with her eyes, warning me about Franklin Opano – oh shit!"

"Yeah, Tom. Big Deb sensed he was a fake. That's why she called me, after I'd been in hiding so many years. That's when I knew that I could finally work to clear my name."

"Big Deb – wait – oh, fuck this, man, wait a minute – my wife and you set this whole thing up? Fuck! And kept me in the dark? That bitch kept me in the dark? I'll kill her, man – and you, you son-of-a-bitch – you're trying to pretend you're good when everybody knows what you did, I'll kill you too, motherfucker!" Big Tom had snapped his recliner forward, stood up to his full six foot three inch old-growth height, and was moving toward Chiuk, his tree-branch-sized arms reaching toward him in a strangle hold, when a female voice stopped him in his tracks.

"Big Tom! Don't! You have got to listen, now, if you've never listened to me before."

The goliath stopped his stomping, stunned. Turning around, towards the entrance to the kitchen, he beheld none other than Big Deb in all her Scandinavian glory and indomitable power moving slowly towards him, arms outstretched, eyes beseeching.

"It was the only way, Tom. After you didn't take my warning – those signals, you taught me so long ago – I went back inside the kitchen and called Chiuk – he'd been in the day before, said he was an old tribal friend of yours, said to call him if this Opo character showed up – and when I could see you were falling into his trap, just like Chiuk said you would – well, that's what I did."

Big Deb stood, solid, like a Swedish castle. "That's what I did, Big Tom. I called Chiuk – and told him that what he thought would happen, had happened." She sniffed. "Hell, man. I knew that Franklin Opo guy was a fake the minute I saw him. But – Tom – you were so taken with that Nancy, that Indian singer gal, and this Opo guy looked like her brother, even to me, and you kept ordering drinks, and then Chief Bigelow showed up, and…"

"Yeah, and then I showed up." Chief George Bigelow politely put his hands on Big Deb's elbows, behind her from the doorway, and gently moved her aside.

"Manta-Ray, Chiuk – good to see you. You look tired. Just sit there. We'll have steaks – potatoes and greens – the whole nine, plus good red wine, in a minute here. Everybody relax."

Chief George cast his big brown eyes at Tom Mooney. "Please sit down, Manta-Ray. That dog is old, and you're making him nervous."

Bigelow turned around to bark a question back through the doorway into the kitchen. "Limen, you crazy pieman, how long until dinner?"

"Oh, maybe twenty or thirty minutes, Big-Fat. Shut up, or explain everything. I don't care what you do. Just don't fuck with my dog or cats – otherwise, I'll kill you, and hang your hide on the barn door."

Chief George Bigelow moved his bulk onto the enormous couch, sitting right next to Chiuk Al-Desk-Eh. As soon as he was settled down, he heaved a great, satisfied sigh, looked at the warm, orange fire roaring in the great grey stone hearth, turned his head to Chiuk, and slapped him on his knee with a hand as thick as an oak trunk. "So, Spreckles Chiuk, is everybody here?"

"Not yet, my elder. We are missing the one they call Cowboy, the one they call Clear Isabell, the one they call Helen Walking Feather of the tribe of the Lummi..."

"I am here, you slimy, secretive sons of warriors. I am here. But, let's make it quick – I've got a two-hour drive back to Lummi Island, and I will not miss the next episode of 'Law and Order'." So spoke a large tribal woman, quite elderly now, known as Helen Na-Esk (Walking Feather), chief Lummi elder, missing none o f her early spark as she was escorted into the room and seated next to Chief Bigelow. "And how are you holding up, you old fortune hunter?"

The sound of a large pickup cam crunching up the gravel driveway. Big Tom started, rose up, and looked out the window. "Well, by God, that's my son, Cowboy. And – Jesus! He's got Nancy with him. I didn't even think they were talking to each other at this point, much less riding together."

"Alright – Tom – let's just get em in here," intoned Chief Bigelow. "Like Limen said – in a few minutes, all will be explained. Or – extrapolated, if you will."

Big Tom rolled his eyes, and confronted his fellow elder. "Where the hell are you coming up with these big words all of a sudden?"

"Well, Manta-Ray, I..."

"Silence, please. Tribal royalty approaches, young and foolish as it is. Chiuk – you will rise with us to recognize their entrance." So spoke Walking Feather, Lummi elder, and to everyone's surprise, Chiuk not only rose off the couch, but bowed to his sister as she walked into the room, totally aghast and completely confused at the gathering she beheld. Her husband's father; a female tribal elder in full ceremonial dress of the Lummi tribe; Chief George Bigelow, her chief elder council and guide; an ancient black Labrador dog, now half-grey and barely able to rise, who looked exactly like her old family's dog from twenty years ago called Bones, and...

Nancy almost fell down. Facing her from across the room was a man, a lean, leathery man, whose face she remembered – whose face reflected her own, shining through years untold – with a stark honesty and outright family resemblance that without thinking, she cried out, "Spreckles! Oh, my god, Spreckles, is that you?" She ran forward, and he took her into his arms.

"Yes, indeed, Thistlebone. It has been so long, so long, my sister."

"Oh, man, oh, brother. Where have you been? Where have you been, my brother?" Nancy drew back, wiping tears out of her eyes. She regarded the rest of the room with sudden disapproval.

"Wait a minute." She faced Cowboy with eyes full of arrows. "What the fuck is going on here? Chief George – Big Tom – Spreckles?"

"My name is Chiuk In-desk-ah, little sis. But you can call me Chiuk. Nobody calls me Spreckles anymore."

Nancy looked abashed. "Of course, Spreckles... I mean, Chiuk. I knew that. But – what is..."

"Nancy, please sit down. Somebody make her a seat – it's getting kind of crowded in here," said Big Tom.

"Hey – I'm on it, Dad." Cowboy pulled a chair forward, and Nancy plopped into it, looking around her like she had just woken up out of a dream. On the side, Helen fumbled a cigarette out of her purse.

"No smoking in here," intoned Dr. Limen, who had just come in from the kitchen. "Who wants drinks?"

"I'll take the usual, Doc.."

"Me, too, Doc..."

"What the usual, Doc?" asked Helen Walking Feather.

"Maker's Mark bourbon, on the rocks or straight up, your highness," answered Dr. Limen.

"On the rocks, then. And – Doctor – could you make it a double? I think I'll need it, after I tell all these gathered here what I've got to say, right, Chiuk?"

"Right, Walking Feather. I'll sit now. I already had a double, but I wouldn't mind another."

"No problem, Chiuk," said Limen. "You are more than welcome to drink, here, at the fire of the elders."

"What the fuck is going on here?" Cowboy demanded. "Limen, come back here. Dad – why are all these people here? Chiuk, you son-of-a-bitch, Helen, Chief George…"

Everyone's ears pricked up as another set of tires was heard crunching up the gravel of Dr. Limen's driveway.

"Ah – that must be Mr. Harry Box."

"Mr. Harry Box? What the hell is Mr. Harry Box doing here? I mean, wait a minute!" hollered Cowboy.

Dr. Limen ushered in a pale-faced man in a rumpled brown suit.

"Everybody, let me introduce Mr. Harry Box. Mr. Box – our gathering will stand and be introduced to you, as is tribal custom. This is Chief George Bigelow, this is Cowboy, a carpenter who is also a cop, this is…"

"Hey, Doc, go back in the kitchen and work on those steaks. We've got it from here," intoned Chief Bigelow.

"The day I take orders from you, you old fart, is the day I start taking orders from Cowboy…"

Suddenly, everyone's ears pricked up again. Another set of tires was crunching in on the gravel.

"Now – who the hell could that be?" asked Limen. "I thought that everyone was here…"

A car door chunked closed, and small footsteps were heard walking up the stairs.

"Hello? Who goes?" inquired Limen.

"I am Clear Isabel," chimed a voice like orange diamonds glittering in the dark. "And I will be your tribal arbitrator." A small, brunette, sparkling woman walked into the room – she had the countenance of a female warrior, yet her brows had a reflection of peace and harmony – as if ancient wisdom had taken flight, and landed on the face of a young woman who had been cruelly wronged, many years ago. And so it was in truth – Clear Isabel was one who was chosen by the elders of her tribe to negotiate treaties between hostile warring factions, and thus attempt to bring about peaceful settlements – or else, advise her own tribe to get the hell out of the way and let the rest of them fight it out amongst themselves.

"I am not here to interfere, or in any way bring influence or judgment. I am here only to witness historical events, as they unfold, and to record them. In the use of that, I have brought a recording device."

The entire room shuffled, nervously. Cowboy cleared his throat – rudely. "Now, listen, little girl. Unlawful and unapproved recording is illegal, and as a Nipsak County Sheriff's lieutenant, I don't think that I can allow..."

"Shut up, Cowboy. You too, Big Tom." Chief Bigelow stared down the two lawmen. "I trained you both in the constraints of the Suquamish tribal law, and then you both busted out and went to work for Nipsak County – I know, I know, the money was better – and better chance for promotion, all of that. And you guys did it – look, everybody, Cowboy's a lieutenant! But, back in the tribe, people – Clear Isabel outranks you in every way. She is a representative of her people – of her tribal nation – and is judged by her elders in the talent and intelligence that she was born with – to witness, inscribe, and otherwise take in these proceedings – and if that includes recording, then so be it. I'm old, and tired, and – to tell you all the truth – I really don't care that much anymore what happens on this earth, since I'm gonna be gone soon – but, Helen Walking Feather reminded me before I cam in here today – that we elders owe one debt to the young ones – and that is, to pass on the truth. In the old days, it was by word of mouth. Now, it is by recording device. I will leave it up to vote. Does the recording device held by Clear Isabel, and the one that we all know is also held by the man known as Harry Box, stay among us or go away? Vote now, by voice."

"They stay," said the voice of Helen Walking Feather.

"They stay – let 'em rip," boomed the growl of Big Tom Mooney.

"Yeah – let it be recorded. But, for the record, I guess I should tell you, that I've been taping everything too. You know I'm a cop on dispatch," said Cowboy.

"OK – I've got to admit that this whole room is wired," rumbled the voice of Dr. Limen as he came in bearing a tray of drinks and crackers. "And all of you can kick my ass for it later. But, don't forget, I was a cop once, too, assholes. Now – let's have a drink – and a toast, to Clear Isabel, who is the most tribal pure, among us – and who will keep peace in these proceedings. Recognize her, now. Strong knives or more will defend this woman from anyone here who attempts to block her from her path – she will be allowed full views and witness – under tribal law. Mr. Box, hold up your hand."

Harry Box looked confused. "What? Why? Which hand?"

"Harry Box are you not here as a representative of the United States Federal Government?"

"Well, yeah, but, wait a minute, let me explain…"

"Mr. Box, you are here, present, on federally recognized Indian reservation land. You are here, with us – American Indian tribal elders. We are about to discuss tribal matters, of which there is a criminal nature, and which involve federal law enforcement. You must raise your hand, Mr. Box."

"Why?"

"Because, Mr. Box – for you to continue to be involved in the discussions which are about to commence – we, as herein described as tribal representatives, must give you a new name."

"A new name? What? Wait a minute…"

"Yes, Mr. Box. Even though we already know that Harry Box – as wonderful a name as that is – is not your real name in life, we, now, in this room, must assign you a new name –and since we're all recording this, your listening agency can assign it as well. Simultaneously. OK, Mr. Box?"

"Well, yeah, sure, I mean, what the hell. What's the new name gonna be? I mean, you know, Harry Box was kind of dumb, anyway, I got a lot of comments, as you can imagine, and I'm just as glad to be rid of it..."

"Your new name, Harry Box, is Hosteen Mellaton!"

Everyone nodded.

"So recorded."

"Hosteen, go sit down, and shut up. We will allow you to record these proceedings, but, you will only speak when you are spoken to, unless Clear Isabel speaks to you. Do you understand, Hosteen Mellaton?"

"I do. I'll sit down. Uh, one thing?"

"Yes, Hosteen Mellaton?"

"Could I have a drink, too? And maybe some food?"

"Surely, Hosteen. Sit on the end of the couch there, next to Chiuk In-desk-ah. Limen! More drinks, more food! Pronto!"

"OK, big mouth! Coming up!"

Now that everyone was seated around the enormous living room, the fire was crackling, and Clear Isabel was alert and focused onto Chiuk In-desk-ah's every speaking word – he continued with his narration.

Chiuk shifted in his recliner, and cleared his throat. A great silence descended upon the room. The maple logs crackled in the enormous fireplace. Old Kloons groaned, shifted his body, and stretched out upon the carpet, sighing.

Chiuk's face took on the hardness of old growth fir, as his eyes stared into a nothingness that was thousands of miles and many years away. Then his eyes swept the room, first lighting on those of his sister, then Cowboy, sitting next to her, then Big Tom, then Chief Bigelow, then the others, finally focusing on Clear Isabel, who gave a small, respective nod.

"I am Chiuk In-deska, a life-born member of the Suquamish Tribe. I also have tribal blood from the Port Gamble S'Klallam Tribe, and white blood from those who shall remain unnamed, for now.

"Years ago, there was an incident up in the Pool-sak hills, where people were taken hostage, and people were shot – it has become known as the Pool-sak incident. Chief Bigelow's family was involved, as was my family. I was blamed, and I vanished. I know how to vanish – there are many places around the Salish Sea where a man who knows rivers, and fish, and trees, and mountains, and has friends on other reservations, can vanish.

"But I was never happy with the result. Those of my tribe – with reasons, thought that I was guilty of those crimes. Those reasons were a lie – and yet, so many believed them, that – I stayed away. I had help – certain people knew that I was not guilty of the crimes of which I was accused. The Lummi, in particular..."

A quick nod to Helen, who nodded back.

"...knew, after hearing me out, that I was wrongly accused. However, I'll tell you now – you that are gathered here, my people – I did not do those things of which I was accused so long ago."

Chiuk's old/young eyes cut over to Nancy's. "Thistlebone, I missed you most of all. I was hiding in the woods, all those years, and now and then I would venture down to where a friend would meet me and give me another CD that you had recorded – and I would go back up into the mountain canyons, in the summer sun, and listen to my sister sing her heart out – when I knew nobody was within fifty miles, I'd pull out my earphones and put my little CD player on speaker and your beautiful voice would lift into the clouds of the western slopes and canyons of the Olympic Mountains, startling eagles and falcons who would fly into circles, higher and higher as your music lifted their wings."

Chiuk looked over at Nancy. Her cheeks were wet with tears, as her eyes shone, looking back at him. Cowboy squeezed her hand, and she squeezed back.

"But, I knew, eventually, I would have to come back and clear my name. I was going to try to get in touch with Chief Bigelow, but, my instincts told me that wouldn't work. So I went to Helen, of the Lummi Tribe."

Helen cleared her throat. "Chiuk came to us, and I called the elders together for a testimony meeting to witness the true-spoken words of a tribal member of our Suquamish brethren. It was shown in the records of Elders, and it was noted that we called the words of Chiuk Al-des-ha the truth. We, the Lummi, stand by Chiuk Al-desk-ah. Although – whatever he has done since then, we cannot speak of with any knowledge. That is our statement. Now, since you're done with me, I'm leaving."

Helen rose up, and nodded to the gathering. "You all know me. Chiuk speaks the truth." She swept her steely eyes. "Now, like I said – I don't want to miss 'Law and Order'. Let's go, Sila-wa."

Helen and her daughter left the room. Everyone waited until they heard the steps down the desk stairs, the footsteps crunching on the gravel, the chunk of the card doors, the roar of the engine, and the departure of the vehicle as it left that part of the forest.

Chiuk continued. "As a kid, I was crazy, confused. I didn't know if I was Indian or white. I was a half-breed, growing up on a res. Hell, a lot of us were. Then, at the school, one kid pushed me too far – he was full-blood Indian, he said I was trash, and couldn't play with them – and I pushed him back. He fell down, I jumped on him, and beat the shit out of him. The teachers pulled me off – called my folks. They weren't around – the teachers told me to walk home, which is what I did. Well, that kid rounded up five of his buddies and they jumped me on Geneva Street – beat me half to death. At least, it felt that way. And they told me – they were all full-blood Indian, and I wasn't, and my folks weren't around, so I should get the hell out – off the res. Said if they saw me again, they'd kill me.

"I went home, and there was nobody there. So I went off the back stairs, into the forest. I was down, down in my mind – I didn't know what I was gonna do. I had a couple of friends, but they were full-blood – and had sided with the others. I didn't have any white friends. There weren't any there. I walked into the woods, looking left and right, in case I was attacked. I didn't know what to do.

"Then I heard a girl, singing. Her voice was like a warm blanket, covering you at night – unexpectedly. It was my little sister, Nancy – who we called Thistlebone. She was sitting in thistle patch, picking thistles out of her dress, singing, laughing.

"I stopped and looked at her. She looked up at me.

'Whatcha doing, Spreckles?' she asked.

'Nancy, did you get into another patch of thistles?'

'Yeah.' She looked up. 'What about you? Are you ok, big brother? Did you get into the thistles, too?'

'Why do you ask that, you little Thistlebone?'

'Well, you look kind of stuck like me.'

'Well, I did get stuck with some thistles, little sister, but I took them out. And now, I think I'm going to get out of the thistle patch altogether.'

'What do you mean, big brother? Are you leaving? Are you going somewhere?'

'Yeah, little sis. I'm gonna take off. But, before I go, I want to tell you something.'

'What?'

'It was your voice, singing in the forest, that brought me here, Thistlebone. And it is your voice which will bring me back home again. Remember that, Nancy Che'al-esk-ah-neh. Your voice will bring me home.'

"She cocked her head, considered, and nodded. Two robins flew into the tree above her and began to sing their song of spring.

'Ok, big brother. Hey – do you think Mom will be mad at me, 'cause I got into the thistles again?'

'Nah, little sis. Don't worry about Mom. It bugs her that you always get thistles in your clothes – but, she thinks it's funny, too.'

'Really? She doesn't laugh that much when she's picking them out of my clothes.'

'She's laughing inside, little sister. She's laughing inside.'

'Oh, yeah. I get that. Ok, Spreckles. I'll tell Mom you left. When will you be back?'

"It'll be a while, Nancy. Now, pick yourself up out of that thistle patch and go home. Ok? I'll see you later, you little Thistlebone. I'll see you later.'"

Nancy's cheeks were running with tears, as were others' in the room. Kloons, the old dog in front of the fire, yawned tremendously, stretched his legs, got onto his feet, and went sniffing over to the front door.

"Oh, shit, people, I hate to bust up this beautiful bubble but Kloons has got to go outside and shit. He can't make it down the stairs anymore, so I fixed him up a shit box over on the far end of the deck. Ok, Kloons, out you go, buddy. Don't be long."

As the old doctor let the dog out onto the deck, numerous voices lauded him. "Hey, have a good one, Kloons. Come back soon." "Good poops, Kloons. Solid!" "We'll miss you, pup. See ya in five." "Be good, Mr. Kloons, don't fall off the deck while you're pooping."

The door closed, and the old dog waddled over to the far end of the deck – out of the lights, into the shadows, sniffing out his poop box. Sniff, sniff, sniff. Wait a minute – I know that scent, it's human – it's from way back – who is that? I'll go closer…

"Hey, Kloons, it's me, Franklin. Remember me, Kloons?"

Kloons wagged his tail slowly, as the scent-memory returned – and then rushed forward, to who he thought was an old friend.

Chapter 24

Franklin Opano. His mind was like a dark river full of tar; the polluted waters flowed swiftly above, between the banks, showing a pleasant, slight green color as the waters rushed by. However, in the sludge buried below, strange thoughts and bad evil bubbled deep in the muck and ruin. The voices were dark and ancient; the rumble of the old clay had become all that Franklin could hear, echoing like the thudding darkness that brought shadows from his childhood – he looked too much like Spreckles.

And Spreckles ignored him, just like all the other half/white cousins that had taken her attention away from him. He scurried into the trees, to hide, and to think. He could still hear their voices, laughing and screeching as they played.

"Hey, what happened to Spreckles?"

"Oh, you know, he ran away, like always. He's probably hiding in the words, like always. Watching us. Always watching us."

But it wasn't Spreckles hiding in the woods, always waiting. It was him, himself – trembling, and then vanishing in his mind – Franklin, who couldn't catch fish. Franklin, who couldn't dance. Franklin, who couldn't play music. Franklin, who couldn't figure out the first thing about girls. Franklin, who ran and hid in the woods when the bulldozers came to rip out a hundred acres of old growth forest to build an "Indian casino". Franklin, who was scared. He fled farther into the woods in search of his old friend; he camped out on hilltops, ran secret signals through the trees, and go no reply.

In his teen years, Franklin went further into hiding. The person people saw when he had to mingle with humanity was just a façade, the same old stone-face they'd known for years. But nobody knew what was inside him, waiting to get out…

He took the old lady on the ridge at gunpoint, in one of his many disguises. After all those cops couldn't gun him down, just nicking his wrist, he fled the res forever and joined the Navy. Further into hiding went the crazy Jack that was really him, further into his evil box. He was promoted, then again a year ahead of time, and crossed over to become an officer. His qualifications were impeccable. He didn't have anything else to do...

Specializing in military discipline, he would sit in with the executive officer on board during captain's masts, where sailors were called upon to pay for their foolish indiscretions while on liberty in foreign parts. Usually it involved restriction to quarters, or restriction to duty station at the next liberty call – sometimes a demotion, a drop in rank, a loss of a hard-earned stripe. On extended home leave, Franklin began to explore the transvestite life – dressing up like a woman, at first in private, then touring the TV bars in states other than his own. The Jack-in-the-box was stirring, getting grumpy – he wanted to unlatch his spring and bounce out, uncoiling, unleashing, blowing his top. But it wasn't quite time, yet.

Assigned as the junior officer to follow through with the disciplinary action upon two sailors involved with drugs in the Philippines, he discovered that they both had ways to trap him in a web of lies and fiction – one was a cross-dresser like himself, and the other liked to watch – but in the course of his investigation, he found enough ways to counter their amateur attempts at blackmail with his own, more vicious attacks. Having access to their families, through Naval personnel records, he quickly nipped their veiled threats in the bud, promoting one as his assistant, and arranging a general discharge for the other.

His new assistant, sporting two stripes on his sleeve instead of an iron boot out of Navy service, quickly became astute at Lieutenant Opano's way of thinking. Individuals busted for drunk and disorderly were quickly shoved aside to the Marine detachment. Two days in the brig, and restriction to duty at the next liberty call. Individuals with drug charges, however, were brought quickly to Senior Grade Lieutenant Opano's attention – especially those with aberrant sexual behavior. These cases the lieutenant dealt with directly – with no Marines involved – and usually removed them from the docket of the

130

captain's mast. With the approval of the executive officer, Franklin brought these sailors into his office- with no one else but his assistant attending as witness. His assistant had a large head, crowned with red hair – and had thus had accumulated the nickname "Pumpkin Head" or just "Pumpkin" from his shipmates. Behind his back, of course – for Yeoman's Mate Second Class Mendhal held considerable power when it came to who would be charged, and who wouldn't – who would do 48 hours under the gun of the Marine brig, and who wouldn't. And nobody wanted to do 48 hours in the Marine brig. No. Nobody.

So, after twenty years in the Navy, Lieutenant Commander Franklin Opano let it be known to the 7th Fleet Command that he wished to resign his commission and rejoin public civilian life. His commanding officer asked him to defer this decision, and take thirty days leave, and consider.

"You've been an outstanding officer , Opano. All the department heads agree on this, including the chiefs. I'll personally sign the papers elevating you to full commander rank, in charge of military discipline aligned with the Naval Judge Advocate. You'll have to go shore side, of course, and serve a few years in the Pentagon. But – it could be a step toward a captain's rank, son. A possible admiralty, if you continued. At the very least, I'd request you back here on this carrier as my executive officer."

"Well, thank you, Captain. I appreciate your encouragement, however, I'm afraid my mind is made up regarding this matter – I am done with the Navy, and I intend to return to civilian life."

"Gonna go to law school, are you, Franklin?" The captain lit a cigar, leaned back, and relaxed. He regarded Opano through the clouds of smoke. "My exec, Wilbergin, will give you full marks. He's got a juris doc, you know."

"Yes, sir, I know. Wilber and I talked about it. But – the truth is, sir – I'm just tired of the Navy. I want to see if whatever talents I have can be more lucrative in the civilian sector."

The captain's eyes went into a scrunch, and he leaned forward, tapping out his cigar ashes. "Your talents? Shit, Opano. You are one of the cleverest officers I've ever seen at sniffing out sailors who are guilty of shore-side offences. The stranger, the better, for you, yeah? Why don't you go to the Pentagon, take a billet in naval intelligence? Shit, you're a natural. I'll back you all the way."

Franklin gritted his teeth, and the sludge at the bottom of his riverbank seethed. He answered, with self control. "Thank you again, Captain. I am going to resign my commission. I've completed the duty, and feel compelled to return to civilian life, and make a go of it there, sir, with the years I have left."

"Alright, Opano. I can see your mind is made up." The captain paused, then leveled his eyes at Franklin. "You are part American Indian, is that right, Lieutenant?"

"Yes, sir – I am roughly half. I was born and raised on a reservation."

"Intend to go back there? Mind you, Opano, that is not my business, once you muster out of the Navy, however – we have a large naval base quite close to where you're from, as you know, and, well – perhaps you'd consider keeping an eye on some of those sailors when they go on shore leave. When an aircraft carrier puts in at Puget Sound Naval Shipyard, it's there for six to eight months, and those kids get apartments, rent houses, get married, get divorced get in trouble with the law – as a matter of fact, Lieutenant, I recently received a dispatch regarding enlisted men in Nipsak County, which is quite disturbing..."

"Well, actually, yes, sir, I would consider shore duty intelligence, as an undercover officer. If my billet could include extensive flexibility, or, should we call it, unilateral command judgment in the field as to how to interact with possible perpetrators..."

"Call it whatever the hell you want to, Opano. Just see if you can put an end to the drug use, or at least put a leash on it. Dig as deep as you want – just remember, Naval Intelligence in port always works hand in hand with local law enforcement. We'll arrange an appointment for you to connect with the appropriate officer regarding the area in question. Ok?"

"Yes, sir. I'm fully on board, sir."

"Very well, Opano."

They all stood, and the captain reached across his desk to shake Franklin's hand. "Let's see if we can get to the bottom of this crazy stuff, and bring our sailors back to the ship in one piece. And, with all due diligence, Opano – I want attention to Navy families. We're on the same page?"

"Yes, sir, absolutely. We are on the same page, sir."

"Very well, Exec, take him out and debrief him as per his legal parameters as an undercover operative in the field. Do not forget the objective, here, gentlemen. We want to nip this drug use in the bud, before it grows worse, and causes more damage to naval personnel, and civilian families. Are we clear on this?"

"Yes, sir."

"Yes, sir."

With a salute, they departed the captain's cabin. Once outside, the executive officer drew Franklin over against the nearest bulkhead. "Look, Lieutenant. This is the weirdest goddamn thing I've ever seen in the Navy – and I've been serving for over twenty years. I'm not going to go on record as your supervisor on this mission – you're on your own. The captain has given you six months to work this detail – and you can do it on your own, that's obvious. But – and I mean but – don't go too far out there with this."

The commander paused, rubbed his chin, looked down the corridor for a moment, then looked back at Franklin with a hard, practiced eye. "Look again, Opano. I've always thought that you were a weird, twisted-up mother fucker. I don't know you too well – I don't think anybody does. Maybe the captain gave you this assignment because he knows that you can go in there and blend in with these freaky – or, maybe he gave it to you because he has the feeling that you will fuck it up, get involved over your head, and get booted out of the Navy on your own – but, I'll tell you this, man. I'll tell you this. I'm not going to lose my career by getting wrapped up in this shit. I want you to keep a daily log of all your activities, and I want weekly updates, and actual face-to-face meetings every month. Are we clear?"

"Yes, sir. Absolutely, sir. I will be there, like clockwork."

"Very good, Lieutenant. I will engage with you at the next set time that we will arrange. Now, you have permission to pack your gear and disembark the ship at 0600 hours. Step back, salute, and we will disengage. Remember, Opano – I will not allow the Navy to be involved any further with a reason to decommission an officer."

… Echo, echo, echo. On down the line.

And now, so many years later, wearing the disgrace of these memories, Franklin called to an old dog that remembered him, and stroked his ears, and rubbed his furry ribs, beyond the lights of those within, on the dark side of the deck of old Dr. Limen's house. "Hey, old hound," whispered Franklin. Let's just take this ugly old collar off your neck, old boy, and put this new one on."

The old dog wagged his tail, and slithered joyfully under the touch of his old friend. "That's right, buddy. Ok – old collar off, and new collar on. Now, I'll just insert this little old arming device, and nobody is the wiser. Right, old buddy?"

Mr. Kloons wagged his tail, and licked the hand of this old human friend, who he hadn't smelled for so long.

"That's right, old pal. Now – go back into the light – go back and see your old friends. Tell them that I love them, with this special gift. I know, Mr. Kloons. I know that you love me, you old dog. Now, give me one last kiss, before you go, old buddy."

Mr. Kloons turned his face up to the old voice that he had known so long ago, and licked his nose. Then, he turned back toward the lights of the house, and his master, and his old family and friends.

"That's right, Mr. Kloons. Go back to them, now. Show them your new collar – I'm sure they'll all love it. Goodbye, my brother dog. Goodbye."

With a last wag of his tail, Mr. Kloons turned away and headed back into the lighted end of the deck, toward the voices of Dr. Limen and his wonderful guests.

Cowboy was tired of listening to all the blather of cops, Indians, lawyers, and fools. He rose up off the couch and stretched, just as the old dog, Mr. Kloons, walked in off the deck.

"Hey, Limen," he hollered. What's that weird collar you got on Mr. Kloons, now? It looks like he was rolling in the mud with it."

Nancy's eyes focused on the old dog's collar as he walked over to her to be petted. "Wait a minute," she said. "This is weird. Is this something you invented, Limen? This is not the collar for a dog we know and love in this family – and hey – what is this chirping, glowing, white thing? Wait a minute – what are these bumps – hey, Cowboy, check this out. This isn't Mr. Kloons' collar – why is this thing glowing?"

Dr. Limen suddenly connected to the words and yelled, "That is not my dog's collar!" just as Cowboy realized that Nancy was leaving over Hoquiam who was looking at the strange, bumpy collar on the old dog which suddenly seemed to glow with an unnatural light – Cowboy launched himself at Nancy, hitting her in the upper shoulders, then flopping with her onto the floor with his back to the dog and her legs in the air as the dog exploded and Hoquiam's last words were – "But, Daddy, it's not his collar!" and the room exploded in light and every eardrum was crushed and fire rushed through windows and doors and Dr. Limen's last words were… "Oh, no, darling – don't touch that!"

Blue penny, you're the liquor in my cup.
Blue penny, you keep on turning up.

You're the liquor in my cup
You're the funny in my smile
Old blue penny,
Won't you stay here for a while.
Blue penny.
Oh, little old, blue penny.

As Cowboy came back to the consciousness, that old song kept playing in his head: Blue penny, oh yeah, little old blue penny. You keep turning up – oh, baby, you're the liquor in my cup.

Cowboy's eyes finally flickered open, and he focused on a leg. He was flat on his back, and a leg, still dressed in its fancy leathers, the design of a young girl, was lying on his chest with smoke coming out of it.

Blue penny,
Oh, blue penny,
You are the liquor in my cup.
Oh, blue penny,
You keep on turning up.
Blue penny.
Oh, my little blue penny.
Now can I spend you
Can I spend you like a dime
Can I spin you like a nickel,
And make you mine, all mine.
Blue penny,
Blue penny.

Cowboy lurched, and a gout of blood spurted from his side. He tried to rise, and his right boot twisted at a weird angle. He blinked his eyes again, and focused on the leg that was lying on his chest. "Hoqi – I got your leg, baby. Hoqi – Nancy, hey – Nancy, tell Hoqi that I got her leg, with those cool new pants that she bought. Nancy – can you hear? Can you hear me, baby? Tell Hoqi that I got her leg – tell her that it's ok, honey. I got her leg."

Cowboy passed out.

The living room of Dr. Limen was a scene of a massacre. All the windows, all the doors were blown out. Blood was everywhere. Smoke and fitful flames rose from what was left of the floor and walls.

Once again, Cowboy awoke. He focused. He rose up on one elbow, and pushed the leg of his daughter off his chest. Then he clutched it back, as he concentrated on sanity. He hugged the leg, with its stylish leathers. Smoke and evil stink rose to his nostrils as he struggled up and sat on his behind. His eyes focused again, and there was Franklin Opano – glaring at him with all the malice and madness of an evil world.

"Where is Palomino?"

"Huh?"

"Listen, you son of a bitch. I will continue this torture upon you and yours unless and until you tell me where the Cinnamon of Palomino is – where is the magical wanderer with a mind of her own? Do you think that we can let her live? We will kill the creatures that live in the forest – and then we will fall the trees – do you think that we can allow you to live?"

Cowboy looked to his left. Amongst the smoke and ruin, he saw the torso of his old friend, Dr. Limen. The head was still attached, looking with a whimsical nostalgia at the lower part of his body, most of which was missing. One of his arms crept toward his hand, and a glowing eye winked at him in a quick warning before the eyelid shut just as Franklin Opano glared him down – and a sound like crushing rock echoed through the room.

"I rule the coming of the new kingdom! All will be as I say! Casinos, malls, freeways, concrete, concrete, and rare roostings for the birds of the billionaires! We shall rule – and we truly, we truly do – pity the fools who can't make it through the lagoon of the lower levels.

You can't touch us
Our bodyguards will cause you to cuss
If you become too familiar
We will have no choice
But to butcher you
Into the fine cults of forgetfulness
And then we'll let you ride
Out into what's left of the countryside
Until we hunt you down
And we'll see you frown
When a smile is all you have to trade
Like it was yesterday."

Cowboy fell back onto the floor again.

Fireworks at night. Hoquiam lay in a tangle, wrapped in dog and human body parts, some of Mr. Kloons furry tail hanging in her mouth. She spat it out, and went back to her inner visions, back to the drive-in movie…

They were watching "Footloose", a replay of an old movie, on a late, dark evening a few nights before the Fourth of July. It was hot, like it sometimes gets in Northwest summers. Her boyfriend had her top worked up around her neck, and her hand was unbuckling her pants. Suddenly the sky beyond the screen lit up with fireworks – and she was watching a better movie, a new movie, after that, as they snuggled down in the front seat of the car...

"Hoqi, honey, I lost your leg. I can't find it anywhere, baby. Shit, I'm sorry."

It was the voice of her dad. She had come to again, and lying amidst the smoke and stench and blood of Limen's living room. Her father's groans were rising to hysteria.

"Where's your leg, Hoqi? Shit, it was right here a second ago..."

She looked down at her legs; they were both there. Propping herself up on her elbows, she looked across the floor at her dad. There was a leg lying next to him, alright. But it wasn't her leg.

She looked over to where the couch was overturned, flickering in smoke and flames. A hand was lying on one of the cushions. Swinging her head back slowly across the room, she paused at the smoking carcass of Dr. Limen, then went back to her father, who had dropped his head back onto the floor. There was another leg partially wrapped around his neck, which Hoquiam realized in horror was that of her mother. She began crawling toward them...

Nancy and Cowboy were sitting in the school auditorium watching Hoqi recite her poem at the Autumn Drama Talent show. She would recite a line, strike a pose, do a little dance sideways, and then recite another line:

"This is called: Family Over Time.

When it's cloudy around here

Which sometimes is always

Sometimes it rains

And my sister cusses

At her muddy shoes when it snows

Which is once in a while

My dad rides along with the tow truck drivers

Hauling sand for fools when the sun comes out
And shines in the trees
Which is sometimes in the summer
My mom sings about the birds and the bees
And what is hers and what is mine
Working in my family over time.
Thank you."

Cowboy's eyes bugged out, and a huge, teary smile was glued to Nancy's face as they applauded wildly with the rest of the crowd.

"That last line had a double meaning, by God!" shouted Cowboy. Did you get the double meaning of that last line, Piglet?"

"Yes, I did, Pig. Our little ham is pretty damn smart. She gets it from her mom, the songwriter."

"And from her dad, the part-time snowplow driver. Hey, Jimmy and Sula, did you catch that double meaning in the last line of Hoqi's poem? Damn, man, she's a genius…"

"Shut up, Cowboy. Here come my son to do a traditional renewal dance."

"Ok, ok, sorry, man."

As the crowd calmed down and the drums started thumping, Nancy and Cowboy's hands found each other, clasped, and pumped up and down together in mutual pride in their daughter and happiness at what they'd brought into the world.

Now Nancy's eyes came open, blurred with confusion, smoke , and pain, her limbs so awkwardly twisted that she couldn't move. It felt like an anvil was sitting on her chest. Then she heard, among the groans and cries of agony, her daughter calling her name in a sobbing voice, over and over…

"I'm coming, Hoqi," she tried to say, but the anvil on her chest would not let her speak. She had to get the words out, get the words out… She began to hum along with the chanting voices rising over the drums.

<h1 style="text-align:center">Chapter 25</h1>

Opano looked down on the house from the rock escarpment above the trees, and began to clench his hands in spasms. "Shit, shit, shit," he uttered. "I should have thrown a secondary incendiary; the fucking place is not catching fire!"

He had thought the impact of the plastic explosive would blow the logs burning in the huge stone fireplace all over the living room, thus igniting the hardwood floors and so on to complete conflagration. But, no – although smoke drifted through the holes, and small flames flickered within, the place had not gone up. He heard the wail of sirens in the distance, woeful, high-pitched moans echoing in and out of the forest, blending in a hellish harmony with the human moans rising up from the ruins below.

"Oh, well. Not all dead, but certainly hurting, what's left of them. Now for the incendiary, while they're sprawled among the remains – they can watch each other burn. Oh, yes yes yes."

He fumbled in his backpack, and gently lifted out a plastic case with a digital screen attached, which blipped on, displayed a line of bright green zeros. After pushing the button to bring the numbers to 15:00, he began to make his way down the steep trail to the back of the house.

"Put this little gadget against a wall, and it will blow up the silly firemen as well, before they can…"

There was a sudden rustle in the darkness, and as Opano turned, he was hit from the side by a ton of brick, and knocked senseless, somersaulting down the hill faster and faster. The plastic case flew out of his hands as he tried to stop his fall, grabbing branches and rocks. He ended up flat on his belly, facing uphill, half his clothes torn from his body, his chin cut and bleeding, his dick literally in the dirt. He thought about playing dad and quickly rejected the idea. Still, he did not move, except for his eyes, which he rolled up to the top of their travel – giving him a two-inch line of sight through twigs, rocks, and gravel of an enormous moon just rising through the pitch black trees of the ridge.

And the silhouette of a crooked, bent-looking man, just starting to pick his way down the rough trail Opano had carved in his own little landslide. Opano began to gather himself, every muscle signing, arms, legs, hands, torso, feet – when the crooked man got to within a foot of so of his reach, he would have one chance, and one chance only, to leap in a great convulsion from the slope he lay on like a fish flipping itself out of the water, to jump his attackers. There was only the one chance, to make a lightning-quick move. There was no way that he'd have time to go for the Ruger .38 pistol strapped in his ankle holster or the razor-sharp filet knife velcroed under his armpit. One chance…

The crooked man came slowly, down the hill, his figure blending with the rocks and trees as he descended the huge lunar reflection rose into the blue-black sky, blotting out the stars and setting the branches of the trees on cold fire. Now only the man's head and shoulders were visible through the twigs and gravel. Sweat was running into Opano's upturned eyes, making him blink rapidly. The sound of rocks and dirt slipping down under the crooked man's boots came sharply to his ears, as well as small branches snapping and the man's heavy breathing. Opano closed his eyes, and prepared to leap free of the earth that held him, now, now, now, one last chance, he's almost here, now…

Abruptly, all sounds of descent down the hillside stopped. Opano rolled his eyes open again, up toward the creases in his forehead, as far up as he could roll them and still see. Bright light, a pin-point beam, almost blinded him. He snapped his eyes shut and let out an involuntary groan.

"An old trick, Opano. You should know better, amigo. I think you sampled too much funny powder with your tranny friends. You hurt some good folks tonight, amigo. Killed a few. But the young ones still live. You missed your target, there. You should have brought a secondary incendiary, burnt the entire shit house to the ground. Why'd you forget to do that?"

"I didn't." Opano smiled. He knew the case was near, and it was almost time. Now, now, now…

Another blinding flash, this one followed immediately by sheets of orange flame rippling into the trees and shading the moonlight with billowing, greasy smoke. A chemical stink rose in the air, along with the smell of burning flesh. At least it was out in the open, this time…

On top of the ridge, the silhouette of an owl was seen flying across the rising moon.

Down below, as the firetrucks pulled into Limen's driveway, they were blocked by all the cars.

"Get that pumper truck in front," yelled the battalion chief. "Run number four mist nozzles through the doors and windows. Hit the roof with solid cascades. Rudy, where's the sheriffs?"

"Right behind us, Chief."

Cynthia's cruiser bucketed into the gravel, followed by Wiley and Fulton, who almost crashed into her.

"Thank God," muttered the chief. "All we need now is a fender-bender. Who is running backup alarms?"

"Billy George."

"Tell him one more engine company, and bring some meat wagons. No major conflags, but we've got a lot of people in there, and it could go up any minute…"

All eyes turned up toward the ridge behind the house as a fiery explosion ripped through the trees, splashing red-orange blood on the rising moon.

"Secondary event, looks incendiary. Rudy, get the county and state Fish and Game choppers in the air, also notify DNR."

"Right, Chief."

The radios were crackling with emergency voices as Cynthia, Wiley, and Fulton ran up.

"We need ten more deputies. This is an active crime scene, and it's hot. Everybody take cover behind the fire trucks. Sergeant, we need security and a defense perimeter."

"I'm on it, Chief. Due diligence will be applied. Consider possible perpetrators still on the scene, armed and dangerous." She turned to her deputies. "Shotguns and vests, you guys. Wiley, radio for SWAT and explosives. Bomb squad, too. Fulton, make the rounds, make sure these firemen don't step in the shit. Keep 'em out of the line of fire – expect a defilade to come down off that ridge. When backup gets here, we'll secure the front door and wait for SWAT. Chief, can you reach the house with those hoses?"

"Yeah, but just barely from here. We'll get the pressure from the pump truck to max, but there's only 500 gallons in this one. DNR's got the big pumper; we radioed for it. Also helo drops – they can scoop water out of Vivian Lake and put out that ridge fire before it gets too damn big, we hope – that sucker was a chemical incendiary, or my name's Mr. Bojangles... Rudy! You got 'em in the air?"

"Affirm, Chief. Also coordinating with state patrol to screen airspace and keep out the press choppers."

"Outstanding, Rudolph." The chief stuck a cigar in his mouth. He never lit 'em, just chewed 'em. Well, well, he thought. What the hell happened here?

As Cynthia's eyes roamed over the cars, blocking the front of the house, her eyes went round as she recognized first, Cowboy's truck, and then, one by one, the rest of the vehicles.

"Oh, shit, Chief! You know who's in there?"

"Belay those mist nozzles," hollered the chief. "We can't get close enough – everybody run straight soakers." He turned to Cynthia, who was now looking at the house with desperate anxiety. "No, Cyn. Who?"

Chapter 26

Nancy sat at the piano in her wheelchair, and finished playing the last chords of "Whoever Knew." As her voice rose with the final chorus, there wasn't a dry eye in the house. Or, rather, in the crowd, since the stage was outside on the event lawn at the Suquamish Clearwater Casino, and the house was the sky, held up by the rafters of the trees and the birds flying down to the waters of Agate Pass carried the musical notes like tiny, winged canoes across the choppy waters and beyond to the beaches and forests of the other islands of the Salish Sea, Puget Sound. A fat, wet, broad-maple leaf fell on Nancy's keyboard as the wind came up and blew more autumn leaves fluttering through the sunlight in a kaleidoscope of reds, yellows, greens, and golds around the people clapping their hands for the band, Thistlebone, who had gone so far away just to come home again.

As Nancy rolled to the front of the stage, the rest of the band came out and joined hands with her – she motioned to Cynthia, who handed her a microphone.

"Thanks, you guys. It means a lot to us to be home again. And – I guess I've finally made peace with the big guy in the big casino in the sky. Or maybe it's just that I've learned how to gamble – never bring more to the table than you can afford to lose."

Putting her hand to her forehead, she shaded her eyes and looked into the crowd. "Is my daughter out there? Cowboy, Wiley? Will you guys come up?"

A hulking figure with two heads, one in a cowboy hat, turned into Big Tom Mooney helping his son, who was leaning on a cane, walk towards the stage. It was obvious, as they lumbered forward, that Big Tom was blind, and that Cowboy had an artificial leg.

Wiley and Hoquiam came down the aisle from the other side. They all made it up the stairs together, to stand behind Nancy's chair.

"Ok, let's get those tribal drummers up here – and those S'Klallam and Suquamish dancers. I know you're here, too – yeah, here they come, look, in all their regalia. Eagle feather fans, and look – we've got royalty here from the seven cedars. Let's get intertribal, folks, and get the singers up here, too – can you say, gimme some fry bread? We're gonna do this one in the memory of those who we lost that fateful night two years ago – Chief George Bigelow, eldest of Elders, most honored and revered warrior of our tribe since Sealth himself; Helen Walking Feather of the Lummi tribe, honored Elder who will forever now fly with the eagles; Dr. Raymond George Clydeus Limen the Third, forever entwined in our hearts and minds; and last but not least, Mr. Harry Box, whose honorary Indian name will now live with us forever – Hosteen Mellaton.

"Now, Clear Isabel, would you like to start us off? Everybody, get up and dance! This is an old fashioned Indian shindig!"

Clear Isabel started chanting over the drums, all the singers followed her, rising and swooping, sliding, falling, and getting up again to soar into the wind like the millions of pages of a book yet unwritten.

Nancy looked toward the very back of the dancing crowd, and spotted the figure she was searching for, the one she had not named. Her face crinkled into a strong, joyous smile, full of the confidence and well-being that comes from recognizing someone of your won blood that has been separated for so long and has finally returned, never to again be broken asunder. She grinned, and waved, as the music and singers and dancers spilled around her like a waterfall.

From the farthest reaches of the lawn, unnoticed by anyone, alone yet not alone, Chiuk Al Deska waved back.

When next Nancy looked up, he was gone.

Chapter 27

Who was the crooked man on the moonlit ridge? Why did he do what he did? Was he Navy, or maybe a Marine? Was he even human? Or of some other tribe? When the fires were finally brought under control, the chemical residue was discovered to be of Department of Defense origin, as was the plastic explosive used to fashion Mr. Kloons' replacement collar. But when had Opano made such a friendship with the old dog that he trusted him so, to let him change his collar?

On dark, moonless nights, when Limen lay sleeping, did he creep up on the deck with bits of steak and chopped liver? As far as everyone involved was concerned, Opano blew himself up with his own incendiary device. They didn't even know about a strange, cooked silhouette of a man who had saved their lives.

Cowboy named his new band The Six Owls, even though there were only five of them. The sixth owl was the honorary one who flew invisibly, heard and sensed, but never seen, the guardian of the hunter and hunted alike.

One night after a gig, he was sleeping out in the old garage room where him and Big Tom used to drink beer. In his dream, he saw Dr. Limen talking to a much younger, more vigorous Mr. Kloons.

"Come on, Mr. Kloons. Show Mr. Pony Boy our new trick. What's on top of the house?

Kloons immediately answered, "A roof! A roof!"

"Right!" Limen gave him a treat, which Kloons gobbled.

Cowboy laughed and said to Limen, "Ask me how my marriage is going."

Limen tilted his head, thought a minute, then barked like a dog and said, "Rough! Rough!"

"How'd you know?"

"Your dad told me."

Everyone talks about everyone behind everyone's back.

Every now and then, Cowboy saw his old Subaru whizzing around town. Once he tried to follow it, but the guy lost him.

Just like an owl.

Epilogue

There is an ancient legend about a spirit known as the Translator, or the Interpreter. If someone became wise enough, or perhaps, by unwise actions, foolish enough, there were translated into the spirit language and never seen again. This language is universal, everyone is fluent in it, even if they don't know it. This spirit was seen drawn on an old rock and pottery shards as the figure of a tall, thin, crooked man.

One morning, the day before Big Tom's birthday, Big Deb whacked him on the back and said, "Shit, tomorrow's your birthday, old man."

"Is it really? That's incredible that you remembered. I forgot."

"How old are you, anyway?"

"I don't know anymore. I don't want to know."

"Well, let's look it up. Or maybe we can call Cowboy, he might know, or…"

"Let it lie. Let's just say: I'm as young as a river and old as the hills."

Deb guffawed. "What kind of crap is that? Some kind of Indian-speak? I'm talking about, in terms of real age, how old are you?"

"Those are terms of real age. Go swim in a river, or take a walk in the hills. Then come back and talk to me."

Another legend says that if you shoot an arrow into your future, and follow your true path, it will lead you right to it. How soon that might be, no one knows. It could be tomorrow, or the day after tomorrow, or next month, or next year. Or, you might not live long enough to see that arrow again. But one thing is sure: if you wander off your true path, and let your feet have a mind of their own, well, then, it will take a lot longer for you to see that arrow again. You've got to stay, and don't stray. If you fall off a horse and he runs away, you might have to wait a long time before you can catch another horse, if one even comes along close enough to chase, so you better...

"Alright, alright, already, Hoqiuam! Will you stop with all these old Indian adages? We just got little Penny to sleep!"

There was a rustle of blankets in the other room, a sleepy sigh, and then a tiny voice called, "Is it tomorrow already?"

Mullenix Ridge

www.ingramcontent.com/pod-product-compliance
Lightning Source LLC
Chambersburg PA
CBHW011152190726
48288CB00010B/3285